Praise for Rebecca Petruck

Steering Toward Normal

★ "Petruck expertly manifests the gruff ways that teenage guys—especially brothers—express vulnerability . . . It's the warm but difficult relationship between Diggy and Wayne that makes this one a purple ribbon." —*The Bulletin of the Center for Children's Books*, starred review

"Petruck's account of country life is never dull as she depicts the strong work ethic of cattlemen and women, along with the universal conflicts between siblings."
—*Publishers Weekly*

"Petruck captures the setting of rural Minnesota well."
—*Voices of Youth Advocates (VOYA) Magazine*

"In Petruck's capable hands, raising a steer—caring for it, loving it, and eventually letting it go—becomes a keen metaphor for the loss of a loved one." —*Booklist*

Boy Bites Bug

★ "A tale that is funny, perceptive, and topical in more ways than one." —*Booklist*, starred review

"The straightforward and uncluttered style will please lovers of the Wimpy Kid series . . . A sure bet for reluctant readers, pranksters, and budding entomophagists (bug-eaters)."
—*School Library Journal*

"An admirable feat that entertains even as it instructs."
—*Kirkus Reviews*

REBECCA PETRUCK

AMULET BOOKS
NEW YORK

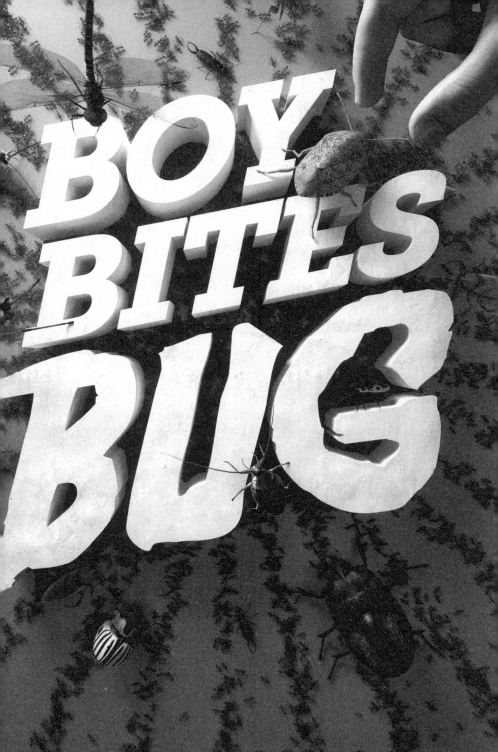

Cataloging-in-Publication Data has been applied for and may be obtained from the Library of Congress.

Paperback ISBN 978-1-4197-3481-6

Text copyright © 2018 Rebecca Petruck
Illustrations copyright © 2018 Mike Heath
Book design by Julia Marvel

Published in paperback in 2019 by Amulet Books, an imprint of ABRAMS. Originally published in hardcover by Amulet Books in 2018. All rights reserved. No portion of this book may be reproduced, stored in a retrieval system, or transmitted in any form or by any means, mechanical, electronic, photocopying, recording, or otherwise, without written permission from the publisher.

Printed and bound in U.S.A.
10 9 8 7 6 5 4 3 2

Amulet Books are available at special discounts when purchased in quantity for premiums and promotions as well as fundraising or educational use. Special editions can also be created to specification. For details, contact specialsales@abramsbooks.com or the address below.

Amulet Books® is a registered trademark of Harry N. Abrams, Inc.

ABRAMS The Art of Books
195 Broadway, New York, NY 10007
abramsbooks.com

To Brandy Elena Garcia and her own
creative culinary pursuits

and

My parents, Teri and Duane, for unwavering love and
support, even when I'm a dork-face

THE INTRUSION OF STINKBUGS CLUMPED ON THE CEILING
in a back corner of the library, a splotch like crusty dried
mud. Every now and then, a few bugs dropped onto the
shiny green plant on the bookshelf beneath them.

Maybe in some schools, the library would have been
evacuated. In Minnesota, with the school near so many
cornfields that it might as well be planted in one, the librarian
had simply left a note on the checkout desk that she had gone
in search of a janitor. After a while, Will Nolan's social studies
teacher went looking for them both. Mr. Hanson probably
wouldn't have left the class of twenty-plus seventh graders
alone if it weren't first period and everyone still half asleep. Will
was tempted to put down his head and nap, too, but instead he
opened the book he'd been carrying around for weeks.

"Is that *The American Revolution for Dummies?*"

Will was a little surprised to see Eloy Herrera beside him.
Eloy was new and hadn't talked much in the two months

since school started. Now he looked from Will to the distinctive yellow-and-black book Will was reading.

"Because that would be kind of awesome," Eloy said.

Will tilted the cover so Eloy could read the title, *Wrestling for Dummies*. "Practice starts tomorrow."

Will had been on the mats since kindergarten and was no "dummy," but this year was different. This year he'd be joining the varsity and JV team, which included seventh-through twelfth-grade students. He'd wrestle with guys a lot older and a lot more experienced, guys who placed at state championships. Will wanted to prove he belonged. The book was one way to make sure he brought everything he could to the mat.

Eloy nodded, then just kind of stood there.

"That *would* be kind of awesome, though," Will agreed. *The American Revolution for Dummies* would be more useful for the paper Mr. Hanson had assigned than the teacher's insistence they use at least three references that were actual books and not websites. Teachers were so old-fashioned.

Eloy gestured at a seat opposite Will, and Will shrugged his OK. He'd taken one of the tables that sat eight so he and his best friends, Darryl and Simon, could spread out. But Darryl had sprawled on one of the couches while Simon poked at the stinkbugs with a metal pointer. Will would be shocked if either of them did any actual work that morning, so while Eloy sat and pulled out his books, Will rested his chin on his hands and went back to his.

Nose in chapter six, "Wrestling in the Right Mindset," he read: *A standard wrestling match lasts six minutes. If you stay focused and mentally tough for five minutes and fifty-five seconds, you'll lose the match in the last five seconds.* Will lost focus that way all the time during matches by thinking too much, caught up in what he *should* do or *should have* done until it didn't matter anymore—he was pinned.

Focused and mentally tough. That was him from now on.

Until the potted plant, the one from the stinkbug hot zone, floated beside him.

He shouted and covered his head.

Simon waved the waxy green leaves near Will's face again, adding a ghostly "ooo" while Darryl laughed.

Focused and mentally tough, Will reminded himself.

Stinkbugs were bad for crops, damaging leaves, stems, and fruit, but they didn't hurt people; they weren't biters or stingers. The smell wasn't even that bad unless the bugs felt threatened.

"Stunts like this are why you're not known for your good ideas," Will said to Simon.

Darryl, Simon, and Will had met in kindergarten and had years of *bad* ideas behind them. Of course, the smack talk would have been more effective if Will's voice hadn't cracked. Stupid puberty.

Darryl smirked, then slapped Will's book closed. "Why are you even reading that? You're definitely making the team."

Actually, all Will had to do to "make" the team was show up and not quit, but Darryl's confidence was still a boost.

"You should join, too," Simon told Darryl. "I'd pay money to see you in one of those bodysuits."

Darryl reached to hook Simon into a headlock. "They're called 'singlets,' and they're not a joke."

Simon ducked away, the plant sprinkling stinkbugs onto the table and carpet.

"Careful!" Will said.

Their antics drew attention from several now-less-sleepy people nearby, including Eloy, who watched Darryl cut left and right to block Simon against the table. But that only made Simon laugh and duck and spin and otherwise fake trying to get away—while still brandishing the bug-bearing foliage.

"Will looks like a Tootsie Roll stuffed into that thing," Simon joked. "One of those miniature ones cheapskates hand out at Halloween."

Darryl knocked him back against the table for real.

"Hey!" Simon said.

Darryl got in close to Simon, chest out. "Will's one of us. You make fun of him, other people will think they can, too." He glared at the onlookers, making them drop their gazes, and landed on Eloy, who only cocked an eyebrow before cutting his eyes to Will, making Will shrug. Darryl got touchy about stupid stuff all the time, and Simon had a knack for setting him off without meaning to.

While Will wasn't wild about being compared to a tiny Tootsie Roll, it wasn't as if Simon was wrong. The Lycra singlets were designed so an opponent couldn't control a wrestler by grabbing his clothes; they were basically a tight tank top and bicycle shorts combined into a one-piece, and no one looked good in them.

"I was only joking," Simon huffed.

"You're always joking," Darryl said through clenched teeth.

"We've got other problems," Will said to distract them and because they *did*: Lots of stinkbugs were on the loose.

The library's large windows let in a creamy, November-morning light that glowed softly on the warm brown of the octagonal table—and now on the gray-brown of the dozen stinkbugs on its surface. They bobbled like weather-worn boats on a calm sea.

Will reached for his book, carefully tilting stinkbugs off its slippery yellow cover.

Eloy pushed back his seat, except the chair legs stuck on the carpeted floor, and he ended up jostling the table.

"Nobody move!" Simon thrust out his hands, dislodging a last few die-hard bugs from the plant, which he finally set down—in front of Will.

"To heck with that," Darryl said. He yanked *Wrestling for Dummies* from Will and made to smash bugs.

They'd all crushed stinkbugs before, on dares or by accident, but usually only one at a time. Will didn't want to find out the nasal damage squishing a lot of them at once could do.

Will threw himself in front of Darryl at the same time Eloy said, "Are you crazy?!"

"No one asked you, *cholo*," Darryl snapped back.

Will inhaled sharply. It felt like the world went into slo-mo.

Darryl's face went red, like he knew he'd crossed a line, but his jaw squared, too—he wasn't taking anything back.

Eloy narrowed his eyes like he planned to cross some lines, too, but Will just looked at the new kid in his jeans and maroon Golden Gophers T-shirt—a weird choice, since most people wore the Vikings' colors, not the University of Minnesota's. He was shorter than Will, which gave him a nice low center of gravity, and he looked solid, kind of shaped like a rectangle. He'd be hard to maneuver on the mat if he ever wrestled. Will wasn't exactly tall, but Eloy made him feel like a beanpole.

Why the heck had Darryl called him a name like that? Will wasn't sure it was actually a *bad* name, but Darryl sounded like he'd meant it to be.

It wasn't as if Eloy was the only Hispanic kid in the

school or even in their class. A quarter, maybe a third, of Triton students were Hispanic, enough that rooms had Spanish signs beside the doors like the one to the *Laboratorio de Computación* right behind him. As far as he knew, none of the Hispanic kids needed the signs; they all talked like everyone else Will knew. Mom said the signs were for some of the parents who didn't speak great English yet, to make them feel more welcome at the school and get them to attend more events and stuff.

The silence had gotten too loud. The entire class was looking their way, and Will felt that he should say something, but his brain was stuck. Darryl was quick to lose his temper and sometimes blurted stupid stuff he didn't mean the way it sounded, but Eloy didn't know that.

"Listen," Will said, though he didn't have anything for them to listen to. He was probably freaking over nothing anyway. Darryl was a decent guy. Look at how he'd defended Will about the wrestling singlet. And Eloy didn't look like he was going to cry or anything.

But it still felt like something was digging at Will's gut.

"Uh, Will?" Simon pointed at Will's chest.

When Will looked down, he was face-to-face with a stinkbug.

IT WAS REFLEX TO JERK BACK, THOUGH WILL COULDN'T
escape his own chest or the stinkbug sitting on it. "We will
not cower in the face of tyranny," he mumbled to himself,
inspired by their American Revolution homework.

"I will," Simon said. "Stinkbugs stink!"

"Then you shouldn't have messed with the plant," Eloy
said.

Simon nodded. "I see your point and raise it an 'Aha.'"

"Whatever," Darryl said, raising a hand to swat the bug
off Will.

"Stop!" Will shouted. It was only a stinkbug, but if it
freaked out and sprayed, he'd be smelling skunk for hours.
Instead, Will inched an index finger toward it and slid his
nail under the front feet. He barely held in a shudder, not
wanting any sudden movements to make the bug retaliate.

"What are you doing?" Eloy whispered.

"Shh!" Darryl hissed, his breath much harder than

Eloy's—and more disturbing to the bug. It darted forward, all the way up the back of Will's hand.

Will jerked at how fast it was, but the bug didn't lose its footing. The tips of its legs were scratchy, like Velcro. Will kept his hand still as he bent his head closer to inspect the bug.

A whiff of something like cilantro and old milk emanated from it, but not strongly. Brown-and-beige–banded antennae twitched at Will from a too-small head resting on extra-wide shoulders. It looked like a miniature football player in pads. Speckles like the dimples on a golf ball dotted its brown body and thick outer wings. Poking from beneath those was another set of wings so pale and thin, they were nearly see-through.

Will turned over his hand slowly, the stinkbug moving in spurts toward his palm. It turned in a circle there, antennae flexing.

"Maybe you'll get superpowers like Spider-Man when he got bitten," Simon said.

"He doesn't need superpowers to stink," Darryl heckled.

"Ha-ha." Will made an effort to grin, relieved that Darryl had cooled off enough to talk smack. But Will still had a stinkbug in his hand. "You'd have to eat one of these to improve your breath," he smack-talked back to Darryl.

"Omigosh, yes!" Simon said to Darryl. "I totally dare you to eat a stinkbug."

Darryl's face went red, which might have been from anger in someone else but which Will could tell was from embarrassment when Darryl darted looks at the people who had gathered around or who were watching from a safe distance. "*Me?* No way. Dare the Mexican. I've seen stuff on TV—they eat bugs all the time."

"Dude, I'm from *Rochester*," Eloy said.

Will didn't say anything. His tongue was frozen in shock at hearing the friend he'd known since kindergarten talk like that. *The Mexican?* What the heck was wrong with Darryl? He knew better than to talk trash about people because of where they came from. Heck, Eloy might not even be Mexican—he sounded like everyone else in Minnesota—but that wasn't the point. Darryl hadn't meant it as a descriptor of where Eloy was from, and everyone around them knew it. Including the two other Hispanic kids in their class, one who had drifted closer to Eloy and the other who was now practically buried in a couch.

Simon giggled the way he did when he was nervous, but it probably seemed to Eloy that he was being laughed at, and suddenly Will was crazy ticked at his friends. They were making the three of them look like prejudiced jerks.

It wasn't right. Will's chest was hot, like he was incubating an alien. He almost closed his hands into fists but remembered the bug in time.

The stinkbug.

The stinkbug that could prove at least Will wasn't a jerk.

"You've been dared, Darryl, so you'd better get your bug ready," Will said. "'Cause *I'll* go first, but you're next."

Then he tossed the stinkbug into his mouth.

EVERYONE GASPED. FOR THAT MOMENT, WILL HAD THE
power of their total attention. He *was* a superhero.

Except.

There was a bug in his mouth.

A stinkbug.

Alive.

And crawling around.

He had tossed it too far, practically down his throat,
and now it skittered onto a tonsil. The feeling made him
gag. He bent over, coughing to dislodge it, while the others
were frozen in shock. It was Eloy who finally tried to help
by thumping Will's back. That's when the bug's defense
mechanism kicked in.

The stinkbug sprayed.

Instinct took over. Will's tongue scraped the bug forward
to spit it out.

Instead, it squished against his teeth.

Will had crushed a stinkbug. In his mouth.

An oily substance coated his tongue. Skunklike fumes stung his throat. His mouth began to go numb, like at the dentist, but not enough to disguise the feel of the crushed exoskeleton, broken legs and antennae, wings, and gooey insides.

Will spat, not caring about the carpet. Or about spreading the smell, which made everyone take a step back and Eloy say, "Careful."

"You really did it!" Simon said, nose plugged but eyes wide with awe.

Will tried to smile, but his throat burned and his stomach flipped like a worm trapped on a hot sidewalk. His voice was scratchy when he said to Darryl, "Your turn."

"No way. It sprayed stink in your mouth!" Darryl waved a hand in front of his nose, backing farther away.

"Stop!" Eloy said, staring at the floor, but it was too late.

Not all the stinkbugs were on the table. A lot had fallen or crawled to the carpet near their feet.

Feet that now crushed at least a dozen stinkbugs.

A cloud of fresh fumes roiled into the air.

Will puked.

TRITON HAD THREE TOWNS' WORTH OF KIDS COMBINED
into a K–12 program in one building with three wings for
the elementary, middle, and high schools. So Will's mom,
who taught kindergarten, got to him fast. And backed away
faster when the smell hit her. Fastest went her sympathy
when she found out he had eaten a stinkbug on purpose.

The library was evacuated.

Eloy was aired out.

Darryl and Simon were aired out and their shoes removed,
planted on the brittle November grass by the front doors.

Will was planted on the frozen grass next to the shoes.

Officially, he had been given his coat, hat, and gloves and
was asked to wait in the vestibule. But the stinkbug stink
was too strong. Whether or not the smell was only in his
head or really did fill the small space between the two sets
of doors into the school, Will couldn't stand it. He went
outside while Mom called Dad to pick him up.

Though they hadn't had their first snow yet, the suggestion of it was all around. Windchill lifted stink off his clothes while air crisped with dry leaves and pine cleared his lungs. Thick frost on the sidewalk had been defeated with salt, and the chemical crystals glinted rainbow sparks in the sunlight. The sight cheered him. Though he had suffered, it had been for a good cause.

Will scraped up some of the deicing salt and sprinkled it into Darryl's shoes.

He wasn't deaf. He heard how some talked about Hispanic people sometimes, but he'd never really *heard* it, not right in his face like that, and not said by one of his own friends to someone in particular.

He spit, then swigged another gulp of orange juice from the bottle the nurse had given him. The skunk taste still burned his throat. He'd almost prefer the taste of his own puke, but throwing up hadn't made a dent. That stinkbug spray was hard-core. Will leaned on the half wall and opened his mouth to see if wavy lines of fumes would shimmer in the air, but the cold only turned his breath to huffs of smoke, a warning it was dangerous.

"Gum?"

Will whipped around too fast. His butt lost traction on the wall, and he started to slide down its bricks, clothes scraping but not catching enough to hold him.

Eloy was fast. He got a foot out, braced against Will's foot to stop his slide on the salty concrete, and he grabbed Will's coat to keep him from tipping sideways. The guy had good reflexes, but he wouldn't have needed them if he hadn't surprised Will in the first place.

"What are you doing here?"

"Thought you might need some gum is all," Eloy said.

"Oh. Uh, thanks." Will took a piece, then jerked at his twisted-up coat and dug his underwear out of his butt, where it had ridden up from his slide.

Then no one said anything for long enough that it got weird.

Why had Eloy come out anyway? Will could see through the glass doors that no one was in the halls, so it wasn't time for a change of class, meaning Eloy was supposed to be in class, too. Had he *skipped* to talk to Will? It wasn't like they were friends.

Though, Will noticed, *his* friends hadn't skipped class to keep him company while he waited for the hand of doom to crush him. Of course, they knew he wouldn't want them to get in trouble for his sake, and Darryl already had enough "visits" with the principal to last through the rest of middle school. That guy. He just couldn't keep from mouthing off. Will sighed another huff of cloudy breath into the air.

"Darryl doesn't mean half the stuff he says," Will said aloud.

Eloy shrugged, seeming as if he really didn't care, but Will couldn't believe it. Darryl might not be, like, a for-real racist—he'd been Will's friend forever—but what he'd said—or how he'd said it, anyway—had kind of come off like he was.

"So, uh, you're from Rochester?" Will said. Rochester was about forty minutes away and a pretty big city. The Mayo Clinic was there, and it was the kind of hospital people came to from all over the country. Will's family didn't go that way often, but he loved when they did, because his favorite restaurant was out there.

Will was trying to be nice and start a conversation to make up for Darryl, but Eloy just gave him a look.

"What?" Will said.

"It's fine to ask."

"Ask what?" But Will already knew and felt squirmy, because even if Eloy had moved to Dodge Center from Rochester, he still wasn't really *from* here.

Eloy rolled his eyes. "I was born in Minnesota, and so was my mom, but her parents are from Honduras. And my dad *is* Mexican. He came to America when he was twenty. So I am part Mexican, and I like it. We go to Oaxaca every year to visit my grandma."

"Cool." The farthest Will had ever traveled was the Black Hills in South Dakota. It was weird to think this guy left the country all the time like it was no big deal. Half the people Will knew had never even left the state.

"You know eating that bug was stupid, right?" Eloy said. "One of the stupidest things I've ever seen in real life."

"Gee, thanks," Will grumbled. It wasn't that he'd been *defending* Eloy, exactly. More like distracting people, because he'd been mad at how Darryl was making things look. But still. Eloy could give him a little credit. "People do eat bugs, you know. I've seen it on TV, too." Just as Darryl had said, though it was mostly on those man-versus-wild shows or the ones about weird food or places to travel. The shows pretended they were educational, about different cultures and stuff, but he could tell from the way the food and people were filmed and the fact the shows were on at all that they were really saying, "Isn't this weird?" And it was weird, and Will laughed and tricked his sister into watching to gross her out. Now *he* was the one grossed out.

He took another swig of orange juice, even though it clashed horribly with the mint gum Eloy had given him.

"I have, too," Eloy said.

Will nodded and looked down the road. He lived a five-minute drive from school. Dad should have been there by now.

"I mean, I've eaten a bug, too," Eloy said.

Will whipped his head around so fast, he might have broken the sound barrier. "What?"

"In Oaxaca, the markets have piles of grasshoppers they sell like popcorn. It's no big deal."

No big deal? "You just said that my eating that stinkbug was stupid!"

"Because it was. The grasshoppers are raised for people to eat. They're cooked and flavored with chili powder and lime. You ate a raw *stinkbug*. Who knows where that thing had been?"

The thought nudged Will's gag reflex, but he swallowed it down. In a place where, when the wind blew from the west, the smell of pig farms was so strong he hid his nose in his shirt, he could *not* let his brain think about where the bug had been.

"Anyway, uh, just wanted to be sure you were okay," Eloy said.

"Oh. Uh, thanks," Will said for the second time, fidgeting with his coat's zipper.

"I should head in."

"Yeah, you'll get busted. No bathroom break lasts this long."

"I'm not worried about getting busted." Eloy fanned pretend fumes away from his nose. "You stink."

Will gave his most sarcastic smile-not-smile, but it only made Eloy grin. As he left, Will's fake smile melted to not at all.

Eloy's was only the first of many jokes and digs Will would get about how he smelled, he realized. Will had never really been picked on by anyone, but then again, Darryl had always been around to defend him. Now? If Darryl didn't say anything? People would hold their noses when Will walked by.

They would clear a path for him, knocking into one another to get away. They would think it was the funniest thing ever. It wouldn't matter that he had known them forever or that some of them stank every day because no one had explained deodorant to them yet. They would all laugh.

Will was the guy who'd eaten a stinkbug.

He slumped against the half wall. Staring at the ground, he saw the skid mark on the salted sidewalk where Eloy had shot out a leg to stop Will's fall. The guy really did have good reflexes, something Will wished he had more of when he hit the wrestling mats.

Will slumped harder. Eloy had come out to check on him, maybe to keep him company while he stank and waited for trouble.

But Simon and Darryl hadn't.

5

"YOU DIDN'T HAVE TO EAT A STINKBUG TO KNOCK ME OUT
with your breath," Dad joked as Will climbed into the truck.

The comment made Will flinch. It was almost the same
thing he'd said in the library, right before Darryl had called
Eloy *the Mexican.*

Dad let the truck idle. "Whoa, you OK?"

Will swallowed. "My throat kind of really hurts."

"Then you shouldn't have eaten a stinkbug."

Will sank down in the seat. "I know, all right? I just . . .
Darryl said something to this guy, and I . . ." Will thumped
his knees against the glove box. "It made sense at the time,
OK?"

Dad frowned, studying him. The truck's engine, still
idling, sounded more and more like someone mumbling
under his breath, the kind of stuff Will didn't want to hear,
like how eating a stinkbug didn't prove anything, and he
was an idiot for thinking it did, and what was he trying to

prove, anyway? If Will was driving, he would have cut off the ignition by now.

After another few seconds that felt like eons, Dad finally put the truck in gear and headed down the school drive, not saying anything.

Dad was a railroad engineer, which meant he had weird hours and could be around to pick up Will at times like this. His route was St. Paul, Minnesota, to La Crosse, Wisconsin, and in a regular car it would take only one and a half hours. In a freight train, it was supposed to take about six hours, but that was before oil started coming out of North Dakota. In stretches with only one track, oil trains took priority, so Dad could sit and wait for hours. Legal requirements meant he could only drive so long before he had to rest a minimum number of hours, so a lot of times he got stuck in La Crosse for a day or two, meaning he could be gone for two or three days at a time. But sometimes he got stuck at home, which could be cool when Will wasn't in trouble.

Except it was cool this time when Dad bypassed their house and went to the small grocery store at the edge of town. "I thought ice cream might help your throat."

Normally, Will would choose a waffle cone caramel fudge peanut mash-up, but he kind of didn't have the energy for it, and he remembered that Mom sometimes used vanilla extract to get the garlic smell off her fingers when she'd been cooking. So he chose vanilla ice cream and tomato juice, because Simon had reminded him that the juice was supposed to work for skunk spray.

Back in the truck, Dad showed him an exchange of texts with Mom.

Dad: *He picked PLAIN VANILLA.*

Mom: *TALK TO HIM!!!*

It made Will roll his eyes but smile a little, too. His parents were dorky sometimes, but they had his back.

Will got away with saying he wasn't ready to talk about it yet because he felt bad and stank. When they got home, Will stopped by the washing machine and stripped. Everything went in: jeans, button-down, T-shirt, underwear, socks, sneakers, and backpack. The detergent bottle glugged as he poured in more than a capful. He had the laundry going almost before his bare butt goose-bumped. After dashing into the shower, Will let out some not-allowed curse words. With the washing machine filling up with hot water, the shower barely trickled, and the water coming out was cold.

Mostly, Will liked his house. It was built in the '70s and had chocolate-brown siding on the top half and graham-cracker-colored brick on the bottom half, so when it snowed they called the house the s'more. It was kind of small, especially compared to Simon's, *especially* for living with two females, but small was good when he was creeped out at night and had to do a search of the premises, like, to protect Mom and Hollie when Dad was gone. It wasn't that *Will* was scared. He wasn't a little kid, though he felt like one right now, shivering naked in the bathtub, waiting for the *ga-chunk-grr-grr-grr* sound of the washer switching to the churn cycle. Finally hearing it, Will slapped on the water again, forgetting it would still be *COLD*.

"Language!" Dad hollered. "You've got soap. Use it on your mouth."

Will was eighty percent sure Dad didn't mean it.

He was far less sure about other things now that he'd had time to think about what he'd done. It wasn't only that at school he'd be the stinky kid. It was also that Darryl was one of his best friends. They caught sunfish and rode snowmobiles out near Darryl's house. They watched scary movies Will's mom wouldn't let him see—movies Darryl turned off when Will got too creeped out and pretended he wanted to do something else. Darryl had taught Will how to shoot an arrow with a compound bow. And Will had seen Darryl cry a couple of times, and not because he was injured.

Friends had each other's back, like Will's parents had his. So whose back did Will have?

Darryl was one of his best friends, but it wasn't okay for him to talk to Eloy the way he had. Most people, probably all they'd really seen was Will eat a stinkbug on a dare. But Eloy and a few others knew there was more to it. Simon and Darryl knew there was more to it, too. Though Will was mad at Darryl for what he'd said, he was still Darryl's friend. But did Darryl think of him as his? Because all Will had seen as he was hauled out of the library was Darryl standing amid the circle of crushed stinkbugs, arms crossed, legs wide, glaring red-faced at Will as if he wouldn't mind squishing him like a bug.

It wasn't as if Will and Darryl had never been mad at each other before. Once things settled down, everything would be fine.

Will filled his mouth with shower water and spat. By this point, it was probably all in his head, but he swore he still had a bad taste in his mouth, and it wasn't only stinkbug.

Will woke to Mom's and Hollie's voices. After his shower, he remembered getting dressed and sitting on his bed to tug on socks, but then he must have conked out. If Mom and Hollie were home, he had slept for hours. He reached for his phone, then remembered it was on the dryer, where he'd set it when he stripped to put everything into the washer. Simon definitely would have texted to let him know what the fallout at school looked like. And if Darryl texted—or didn't—Will would know what the fallout with him looked like, too.

Will needed his phone.

But he was kind of afraid to go out there and get it.

Partly because once he checked his phone, he would know for sure that all the worst things he expected were true. He wasn't generally Mr. Negative, but he had *eaten a stinkbug*. Stunk up the library. And, for bonus points: puked. He probably hadn't even imagined the worst things yet.

Partly it was because Hollie was out there. The thing with having a sister only one year older was that she was in the same school. Well, everyone from three *towns* was in the same school. Triton kept the elementary, middle, and high school students pretty separate, but the middle school was only one long hall, so Hollie was around all the time, and everyone knew he was her brother. There was no way someone, a bunch of someones, hadn't already told her various versions of what had happened. She was probably waiting right outside his door to tell him how bad it was and make fun of him. Heck, he was surprised she hadn't barged in already.

And the last "partly" was because Mom was out there, too. It wasn't that she was mean, but she usually found the one thing to say to make him feel the crappiest. She didn't try to make him feel bad, exactly; she was just always teaching, wanting him to learn from his mistakes. He hated it. It was much easier when Dad got mad and yelled at him to shovel snow off the sidewalk or clean the gutters or whatever.

The worst part was, Mom was always right. Just once Will would love to *not* learn anything, to just be grounded and gripe with his friends about it—the end.

He heaved a giant sigh, then heaved his butt off the bed. Hollie was not waiting outside his door, and that inspired him to try to sneak past the kitchen, but there was no sneaking in their house. It was a simple rectangle with three bedrooms and a bathroom in one half, the living room and kitchen in the other, with the small alcove for the washer and dryer on the far side leading to the one-car garage no one ever parked a car in.

"How you feeling, bud?" Dad asked, essentially ratting out Will before he'd barely cleared his bedroom door.

"I told them what happened," Hollie said.

Will squinted at her. It was confusing sometimes, because she wore a lot of pink workout gear, which seemed so girly, as if she didn't really work out, but he knew she busted her hump at volleyball. He'd been to her games. She hadn't showered yet, and since that was usually the first thing she did when she got home from practice, making the house smell like her fruity, flowery soaps and lotions, she must have spent all her time telling Mom and Dad all the crap she'd heard at school. The betrayal stung, but who was he to complain? Darryl probably felt the same way.

"Mom was the first one they called," Will pointed out, so she had known what happened and had obviously told Dad. All Hollie would have to add were whatever gory details his social studies class might have passed along.

She sighed as if he were Mr. Stupid. "About the new kid."

"Eloy didn't do anything." Maybe Will hadn't woken up all the way, because he wasn't sure what she was getting at.

Hollie exchanged one of those looks with Mom that meant something in girl language.

"I heard from someone that maybe Darryl was being a jerk, and—"

"Darryl's not a jerk!" Will burst out before Hollie finished talking.

"I said, 'being a jerk,'" Hollie repeated, but he barely heard her.

"Is that what people are saying?" Holy crap, it was worse than he thought. He ran for the dryer and his phone, but it wasn't there. "Hey!"

"No phone, and you're grounded for two weeks," Mom said.

"That's forever! And I was only trying to help someone!"

"Whether or not you were trying to help, your stinkbug stunt got the library shut down."

The library was shut down? He thunked into a seat at the kitchen table. This was seriously bad on a whole different level than he'd expected. Though he felt a tinge of injustice about having the library thing pinned on him—*he* hadn't been the one who started messing with the stinkbugs—it was outweighed by the idea that people might be saying bad things about Darryl. Will couldn't let that stand. Darryl would never let that stand if the talk was about Will.

He *had* to see what Simon had texted him.

"Please just let me check my phone *one time*," Will pleaded. "I need to know what's happening."

"It doesn't matter what other people might think," Mom said quietly, putting a hand on his arm as if that was supposed to reassure him. Why did parents always say stupid stuff like that? Of course it mattered what other people thought. He had to spend most of his day with them every day until he graduated high school!

"Anyway, all they're really talking about is you eating a bug," Hollie said.

"Whatever Darryl did or didn't say," Mom said, "I'm glad you tried to show him that being prejudiced isn't OK."

Ick. Will was not "a good role model." He ate a bug! And Darryl would hate, as in detest, the idea of needing to be taught how to be a decent person by anyone, let alone Will.

He put his head on the table.

"It's not that bad, dork-face," Hollie said, giving him a pat on the back. He supposed she was being nice, but it might as well have been trying to light a match in front of a tornado.

Then he thought of something else: The first day of wrestling was tomorrow, and it was one hundred percent guaranteed the high school guys had heard he'd eaten a stinkbug and puked. So much for starting off on the right foot.

Mom said more stuff, but Will's ears buzzed. He didn't really hear anything until "I want you to really think about better ways you could've handled the situation."

As if he wasn't already. He should have stayed out of the whole thing. Eloy looked like someone who could take care of himself. And it wasn't that Darryl and Simon were bullies. They were just being stupid. Will had overreacted, and look what it had gotten him: grounded, phone taken away, probably the whole school making fun of him, even guys from the high school hearing about it. Wrestling practice those first two weeks was hard enough without knowing all the older guys were laughing at him. And Coach. Coach Van Beek was his health *and* P.E. teacher. He'd definitely heard about the stinkbug. Would he think Will was too stupid to be on his wrestling team now?

The day had started so normal. But it had gotten chased around the mat and pinned like a lightweight taken down by a heavyweight.

USUALLY, WILL TOOK THE BUS TO SCHOOL SO HE COULD
get an extra fifteen minutes of sleep, but today he rode in
with Mom and Hollie. Simon went to school early for cribbage club, so he'd be there to give Will the lowdown before
he had to deal with anyone else.

The ride in was dark and gray. Clouds hung so heavy, the
sun would have a fight to rise. Diesel fumes tainted the air.
Will told himself that that was why his stomach was queasy.

But walking into the redbrick blocks of school, he
couldn't pretend he wasn't worried. The diesel should have
ruined his nose for at least a few minutes, but he swore he
still smelled stinkbug. Will stopped abruptly and turned
around in front of Hollie, basically making her bump into
him. "Do I smell?"

Hollie nudged him back with one fingertip on his chest.
"Always."

"Hollie," Will groaned.

"You're a boy. It's basically your job to stink."

"You're not funny!"

"Yes, I am." Hollie laughed.

Will stomped ahead, but they were going to the same place, and Hollie was taller, so she kept pace while hardly trying.

She caught Will's arm and turned him around in front of her again. "Honestly. You're fine. I wouldn't let you come to school stinky."

Will could tell she meant it, which helped a little, but then he faced the hallway again. The school colors of gray and maroon were great when facing an opponent, but right now *he* felt like the opponent. The floor was light gray, and the cinder-block walls were cream-colored. But beneath the fluorescent lights the glossy painted lockers gleamed bloodred like a fresh cut.

When Hollie patted his shoulder, he flinched.

"I won't pretend today's not going to be bad," she said. "But eventually this will be a funny story you tell."

Though she didn't get that it was already a funny story for *other* people to tell, it was kind of nice of her to try to encourage him. Her sincerity triggered a knee-jerk reaction to make a joke at her expense so they could stop with all the feelings stuff, but he held it in, mumbling only, "Thanks."

She grinned as if she knew exactly what was going on inside his head, and patted his cheek before he could duck away. "Good luck, baby brother."

"Thanks, old lady."

She flipped her shiny brown ponytail at him as she walked away. Even when she didn't get the last word, it seemed as if she did.

Will took a deep breath, noticing he *could* because his chest wasn't so tight. Until Simon crashed into the locker next to Will and gave him a heart attack.

"What the heck?"

"Your parents took your phone?" Simon panted.

"Yeah. I guess it's really bad?" Simon's dramatics were certainly not a good sign.

"Are you kidding? It's awesome!" Simon slung an arm across Will's shoulders the way wrestling coaches sometimes did when they discussed strategy before a match. "It's like a fart. You can't talk about it if you haven't smelled it. *Everyone* went out of their way to smell it."

"That's not awesome," Will groaned. He knew. He'd smelled like stinkbug all day and night.

"How can you be twelve and not understand how the social system works?" Simon asked with exaggerated despair.

He was so over the top, Will almost laughed. But people were beginning to trickle in and look at him funny. "I get that I'm going to be the stinky kid and a social outcast."

Simon slapped his knee in exaggerated hilarity.

Seriously? He was supposed to be Will's friend, but sometimes he was so busy laughing, he forgot the friend part.

"Is Darryl ticked?" Will asked, partly to stop Simon's laughter and mostly because Darryl's bus would get there soon.

"I mean, yeah," Simon admitted. "You kind of showed him up with the whole stinkbug thing, and everyone's talking about it."

Will sighed. He hadn't meant to, like, embarrass Darryl. Darryl could be kind of tough sometimes, but that's what made him a good friend. Simon was in *cribbage* club, for Pete's sake. Darryl had a compound bow and had taught both Will and Simon how to use it, which was supercool for fun, but Darryl actually hunted with it and had shot a deer before. The three of them had always kind of balanced one another out.

"I said something to him, too," Simon said.

"What do you mean?"

Simon shrugged. "About it not being cool. What he said to the new kid."

Will's eyebrows could have shot up off his head. It had never occurred to him to just *say* something to Darryl. He'd been so mad, and, come on, it wasn't like they ever talked about *feelings*. But before Will could ask Simon how *that* went, someone cleared his throat. Will turned as Eloy said, "Hi."

"What are you doing here?" Will didn't mean it to sound mean. It was more that he was startled, since they'd practically just been talking about him. Though none of this would have happened if Eloy hadn't talked to him in the library—or if Will had simply kept his mouth shut.

"His ears were buzzing." Simon thumped Will's arm. "Get it? I said 'buzzing' instead of 'burning.'"

Will and Eloy rolled their eyes at the same time, almost as if they'd planned it. Or were friends.

Will sighed. "So, do I have to become an evil genius now?"

"Nope," Simon said. "You're Bug Boy."

"What?!"

"I had to think on my feet!"

"I get the feeling that's never a good idea," Eloy said.

Will snorted before he caught himself. That was a decent burn.

"At one point I heard someone say 'Stink Man,'" Eloy added. "Bug Boy's probably better."

"See?" Simon raised his arms in triumph. "My brains saved the day."

"Your brilliance knows no bounds," Eloy deadpanned.

Simon grinned and strutted in a circle.

Will was confused. Simon seemed to think being Bug Boy was a good thing, which Eloy seemed to confirm. And those people who were looking at him funny started to give him head nods and thumbs-up. Then someone yelled, "You having French flies for lunch?"

Without missing a beat, Simon called back, "Naw, Bug Boy's having maggot-aroni and fleas."

"No, he should have a bee-rito," someone else said.

People laughed, and others shook their heads at the antics but smiled, too.

"Omigosh," Will said. "Is this what people did all day yesterday?"

"Pretty much," Eloy said.

"I spent all night thinking up bug-food names," Simon said. "Fried lice, flea loaf, pot roach, wasples—"

"Wait, what?" Will said.

"Like waffles, but with wasps."

That wasn't actually what Will meant. His head felt floaty, and his ears rang.

He had been worried about getting teased and called names, and that was definitely happening, but not in the way he'd thought.

Will looked at Simon and Eloy, both telling him that things were all right.

He did the only thing he could: He grabbed Simon in a headlock and dragged him to the ground while Simon dramatically played the wounded hero.

Eloy watched them for a few seconds, then said, "You know, some men just hug each other."

Both Will and Simon froze, blinking at him. "What, like, in Mexico?" Will asked.

Eloy rolled his eyes. "Anywhere, idiot."

Will looked down at Simon's head under his arm, then tightened his fake hold. "Well, this is Minnesota. You want to get in a few kicks or not?"

Eloy pretended to kick Simon a few times until Mrs. Olsen shouted at them to keep it down.

Then Darryl arrived.

7

WILL COULDN'T READ DARRYL'S EXPRESSION AND
decided to go with that being a good thing, because "mad"
Will would definitely recognize.

Darryl was tricky. He could get mean, but sometimes
he'd have this look in his eyes, almost as if he couldn't quite
control himself and wanted someone to stop him. Maybe it
was only Will seeing what he wanted to see, but he'd known
Darryl as long as he could remember. Darryl didn't have a
lot of other friends, unlike Simon, who had cribbage club,
and Will, who had his wrestling buds. So Will was pretty
sure Darryl didn't want to lose any friends over a stinkbug.
Will just needed to get Darryl back on their side of the line,
so the story could be funny from all angles with no one
playing the bad guy. But heck if he knew how to do that.

Darryl's gaze shot between Will and Simon—and Eloy—
and settled on Will. Before he could say anything, though,
Simon slung an arm over Will's shoulders again.

"I already gave Will the good news that we don't have to drop him like the booger-eating freak he was in first grade."

"Hey!" Will protested.

"Oh, fine," Simon conceded. "*And* second grade." He grinned at Will. "Darryl and I were just glad you never discovered ear wax."

"Ha-ha," Will grumped, but he squinted at Simon. Will didn't give him enough credit. With one sentence, he had called out what Will, and probably Darryl, was worried about *and* reminded everyone about their history as friends. The joking dig at Will's previous eating adventures didn't hurt, either, though Will had *not* eaten boogers—he didn't think. Like, eighty percent sure.

"But now that I think about it," Simon pondered aloud in exaggeratedly deep thought, "the fact that you *didn't* discover ear wax probably means you never cleaned your ears." He grabbed at Will's. "Omigosh, what does it look like in there?" He stood in front of Will, speaking too loudly with excessive mouth action. "Can you hear the words that are coming out of my mouth?"

Darryl shook his head at Simon's antics, cutting a look at Will to see if he was doing the same. Which Will promptly did, adding a little smile that Darryl matched. Will breathed out, glad they were at least acting normally, and then someone shouted, "Bug Boy!"

Darryl's shoulders tensed halfway up his neck. "You shouldn't let them call you that."

"I know, right?" Will tried a laugh. "It's kind of screwy. I bet I'll hear it every time I walk into the library for *weeks*." He hoped he would anyway. It was cool being cool.

Darryl peered at him. "You know the library's closed the rest of the week, right?"

The rest of the week? That was four days including yesterday! Mom had mentioned the library was shut down, but he'd thought she meant for the *day*. "Why didn't the janitor vacuum up the bugs, spray some air freshener, and call it a day like everyone else does?" Will protested.

"Legal stuff." Darryl shrugged. "They can't spray pesticides with students around, or they need time to air out the room, or something."

"They don't want us growing fins and a second head," Simon said.

"*You* with two mouths?" Darryl said to him. "Civilization would collapse."

"Are you kidding? Simon squared would be magical!" Simon said.

While the two of them debated the pros and cons of Simon having a second head, with Darryl's argument including the apocalypse and global hearing loss and Simon's argument including unicorns, aliens, and Salisbury steak, Will pretended not to notice that Eloy had drifted away. The fact of it dug at his gut, though.

Will had wanted things to be normal with his two best friends, and they seemed to be. But it felt a little like there'd been a price, and he wasn't sure how much he'd paid.

The morning was filled with high fives and fist bumps. People gave Will piles of snacks to hold him over until lunch so he wouldn't have to eat more bugs. Others suggested "lice crispy treats," "spag-ant-i and mothballs," and lots of "French flies" until Simon said they'd heard that one a thousand times and told them to get more creative.

Even people who gave him crap about eating a stinkbug did it to be in on the joke. They plugged their noses when he was near, pretended to eat books and pencils and backpacks, and several people who only meant to pretend to fart accidentally let out real ones, which made some run away and others stop to smell, noting, "Nope, Bug Boy's is worse."

It didn't take Will long to adjust to his new celebrity status. He walked the halls with Simon in the lead doing what Simon called "crowd control" but was really more like his being the "town crier." It was awesome.

Will had gone to sleep convinced of his doom and woke up famous.

"You've got to nip this crap in the bud," Darryl muttered when they got to science class. He thunked into his seat hard enough to make the chair legs squeal.

"But our fans love us!" Simon proclaimed, opening his arms to let the love pour in.

Will had to admit, he didn't want to nip any buds. He liked being popular, and he didn't get why Darryl was mad about it—until Eloy walked into the room. Bug Boy existed because of Eloy and Darryl. No one seemed to be thinking about that part. But Darryl was.

Looking over at Eloy, Will wondered if he should be, too.

Had anything changed other than Will's popularity? No one had apologized to Eloy. Not even Will, really. He was still friends with Darryl and Simon, which was a good thing for him. Eloy was still the new guy, though more people seemed to know who he was, looking at him in ways that were hard for Will to interpret. They weren't mean looks, but he wasn't sure they were friendly, either. Cristian and Tyler, the other two Hispanic kids in class, had taken seats right behind Eloy, making that digging feeling return to Will's gut. He glanced at Darryl.

Darryl was one of those people who could look older and younger at the same time. He was outside a lot, so even though it was November, his face was still pretty tanned, and he was more filled out than most of the other seventh graders. But he had round cheeks and really blue eyes that made him seem cheery and innocent even when he wasn't. No one who knew Darryl fell for the innocent look anymore, because his history hung off him like a cape, though Will sometimes wondered if Darryl *did* get away with stuff. Will worried that Darryl had gotten away with something yesterday.

But then Joshua said something to Eloy that made him smile, and Mackala and Megan bypassed their usual seats up front for ones next to Eloy, saying hi before getting out their books as usual.

Will exhaled, not having realized he'd been holding his breath.

SCIENCE WAS WILL'S FAVORITE CLASS. PARTLY BECAUSE
he liked the stuff they were learning (not that he'd admit
the periodic table of elements was hypnotic to him) and
mostly because the teacher, Mr. Taylor, was also one of the
assistant wrestling coaches.

But today, seeing his teacher and hoped-for coach was
like a knock upside the head. The first wrestling practice was
today, and Will had meant to be in the zone all day: visualizing
moves, thinking through past matches, breathing. Instead, he
was on a freaking roller coaster, first predicting social doom,
then being crowned Bug Boy. Last night he had tried reading more from *Wrestling for Dummies*, but all he remembered
were the words he'd read in the library right before things
went screwy. *Focused and mentally tough for the entire six minutes of a match or you can lose it in the last five seconds.*

The first practice hadn't even happened yet, but Will's
head spun as though the last five seconds of his match had
come and gone—and he hadn't even noticed.

He glanced at Eloy but quickly looked away. "Breathing" had been on Will's to-do list for today. He reminded himself to do it now, and he focused on Mr. Taylor. Will was extra good about doing his assignments and paying attention in class so his future coach would know he was a hard worker. Will got a little jolt when it hit him that Mr. Taylor might think of him as Bug Boy now, instead.

Which was confirmed when Mr. Taylor announced, "Our intrepid Mr. Nolan inspired your next assignment."

Heads swiveled in Will's direction. Butts shifted in seats. For the first time that day, Will got a few looks of uncertainty, even of annoyance. He didn't like it at all.

Mr. Taylor drew a large circle on the whiteboard and labeled it *Biodiversity*. He then marked off five tiny slices: *mammals, amphibians, reptiles, birds,* and *fish*. The giant remainder he filled in with *invertebrates, mostly insects*.

As soon as the class saw the word *insects*, they groaned around laughs and acted as if they weren't excited to be included in one of the funniest events of the school year.

"Usually this class presentation is—"

The class groaned again, with feeling this time. Teachers and their *class presentations*. They loved to torture students with *class presentations*.

"Usually this class presentation," Mr. Taylor said firmly, quieting everyone, "ends up with students choosing mammals like lions, dolphins, or deer. But as you see"— he indicated the five small slices that barely took up any space in his chart—"that ignores the most populous group of living creatures on our planet."

He went on to tell them to choose an insect to study, identify its characteristics and its role in the environment and biodiversity, including its impact on humans, with presentations to begin the week after next since the library wouldn't be open again for them to do research until Monday.

He *also* explained that while the assignment *was* a serious element of their segment on biomes, biodiversity, and ecosystems, he wasn't above using a student's poor decision to generate enthusiasm for his lesson plans.

The class hooted approval, and Will knew that whatever "poor decision" he made next had to be a good one.

WILL COULDN'T HELP IT—HE KEPT LOOKING OVER AT
Eloy, expecting Eloy to be looking at him. Mr. Taylor had as
much as said that Will's bug eating was the reason for the
assignment, and Eloy had told Will about eating bugs at his
grandma's in Mexico. The logical conclusion was obvious.
Eloy would help Will concoct a plan that involved bug eating—on purpose this time.

But Eloy didn't look back at Will.

Darryl did, though.

Will didn't like the feeling of being "caught" looking at someone, especially considering that Darryl hadn't
really been "caught" for his behavior yesterday morning—
especially considering that Will was the only one who'd
paid a price for Darryl's prejudiced behavior. The fact was,
Will was Bug Boy whether Darryl liked it or not. So if Will
needed Eloy's help, Darryl would just have to deal with it.

But first Will had to get Eloy on board.

So Will balled up a corner of notebook paper and chucked the pea-size missile at Eloy.

It hit his head and stuck there like chewed gum, glaring white in Eloy's black hair. Eloy swiped it off, looking back.

Will mouthed, "Wait for me after class."

Instead of nodding, Eloy glanced at the grinning Darryl, then faced front again.

The back of Will's neck heated up, the burn curling over his ears when not only Cristian and Tyler but also Mackala and Megan frowned at him.

He hadn't meant to look like he was picking on Eloy. He'd just needed to get the guy's attention.

Will slumped low in his seat and waited for class to end.

When it did, he told the guys to go ahead because he wanted to ask Mr. Taylor something, glad to see that Eloy seemed to be holding back, too. At least he'd gotten the message.

But when almost everyone had filed out, Eloy stomped over to him. "Don't throw crap at me."

"I know!" Will winced. "But you weren't looking over, and I was trying to get your attention."

"'Hey, Eloy,' would have worked fine."

"I don't talk in Mr. Taylor's class! He's a wrestling coach! I pay attention."

"Throwing stuff at me is paying attention?"

Will huffed out a breath. *This guy* . . . Will had already helped him once. He had to know that Will was one of the good guys. "Are you going to help me or not?"

"Help you with what? You haven't asked me anything."

It seemed so obvious to Will, he was surprised he had to spell it out. "I'm going to give the best class presentation in the history of Triton."

"It's a class presentation," Eloy deadpanned. "It can't be the 'best' anything."

"Are you going to let me finish or what?"

Eloy didn't leave, so Will explained. "Bugs."

"Bugs." Eloy did not look as impressed as he was supposed to.

How was the genius of Will's plan lost on this guy of all people? Maybe Will didn't exactly have a *plan* yet, but he knew it would involve bugs and eating. And then he had it. It came to him like lightning, and saying the words out loud made Will feel electric. "We're going to feed the class bugs."

It made sense, because at the moment, Will was the one who had eaten a bug, and that made him special—for now. But if the tide turned and people started to think it was gross, as he'd predicted yesterday, because it had been gross, then he'd be *the only one* who'd eaten a bug, out there alone, flapping in the wind. But if other people ate a bug, then they couldn't say anything, *and* he'd still be the one who did it first.

He was a little in awe of himself. This really was going to be the best class presentation ever.

All Eloy said was, "We?"

"You said your grandma cooks crickets."

"Grasshoppers. And, no, I said they sell them in Oaxaca."

"Well, can she get some for us? It's not that far to ship, is it? Mexico's just over the border." The post office had those Priority Mail boxes. Would they work from there? And how long did grasshoppers last? Just because he'd eaten a stinkbug didn't mean he wanted to eat a grasshopper that had gone bad.

"Do you pay any attention to the geography and culture segments in Spanish class?" Eloy asked.

"Huh?"

"Mexico is a country like the U.S., and Oaxaca is a state. In the *south*. Not everything in Mexico is 'just over the border.'"

"Oh, uh, I didn't mean that the way it sounded."

"Uh-huh."

"I'm sorry." Will sighed. He hadn't meant to be rude, but his mouth had moved faster than his brain, and now his brilliant idea was going down the toilet. Maybe he didn't need Eloy. Will had latched on to the idea of using him because he had actually eaten a grasshopper before, but Will could probably figure out how to get some on his own.

"My dad might help," Eloy said, catching Will off guard. "Since it's for school."

"Really?" Doubt colored his tone. Eloy had just called him out for being jerk-y, so why would he help, except maybe to set him up to look stupid?

"But I want something, too," Eloy said.

"Ah." That was fair, though as his excitement flashed anew, Will couldn't think what more the guy could want. He was already going to supply the key ingredient for the coolest event to hit Triton since *ever.*

"I think I want to try wrestling. You can help me get up to speed."

The thought shouldn't have been as deflating as it was.

Will remembered thinking a couple of times that Eloy might make a good wrestler, but the prospect of him really doing it felt different. Teammates had one another's back in a way that was different than with friends. It wasn't that they hung out together all the time, but if they saw one of their guys in something it looked like he couldn't handle, they'd step in. Will had kind of already done that with Eloy, and it had turned into a thing. Plus, what if Eloy ended up being better than Will?

He asked Eloy, "How much do you weigh?"

"How should I know?"

The guy didn't even know his weight class. Will held out his right hand.

Eloy hesitated before shaking it. "I help you with the grasshoppers, you help me practice wrestling?"

"Yup." When Eloy hit the mats the first time, it was going to be like taking a hit. He'd probably quit the team before they had their first match. Meanwhile, Will would turn Bug Boy into Bug King. He had nothing to worry about.

10

THE FIRST DAY OF WRESTLING PRACTICE WAS THAT afternoon.

Walking the hallways to the high school wing and the guys' locker room with Eloy, Will felt a little puke-y. He knew, or at least knew of, a lot of the guys from when they'd wrestled in K–6 programs. But this was a real team now, JV and varsity. Though he wasn't sure his nerves were entirely about being the youngest on a team of mostly high schoolers.

He'd heard the call Eloy made to his mom about joining wrestling and having to stay after school. Eloy had made the deal with Will about wrestling, but he hadn't remembered that practice started the same day. His mom must not have been excited about the idea, because at one point while he was talking with her, Eloy stuck his head into his locker and switched to speaking rapid Spanish. He clearly didn't need Spanish class, but when he hung up and Will called him out on going for an easy A, Eloy only shrugged and said he spoke Spanish fine but didn't read and write it as well as his mom wanted.

Now Will wondered if he should have offered to give the guy a ride home after practice, but he wasn't trying to be friends with Eloy. Will *had* friends. Today had been pretty much normal, even if Darryl was maybe still a little mad. Hanging around Eloy wouldn't help.

Opening the door to the locker room knocked Will's attention from his thoughts to his nose. That sweaty-feet funk was too strong to ever get used to.

The locker room was the same one they'd gone to that morning to change for P.E. class, with rows of maroon lockers on three walls and in the middle a stand-alone row of cubbies. To one side was the group shower, its three pillars ringed with shower heads.

But now the room wasn't filled with seventh-grade boys as gawky as Will. It was filled with guys who looked like men.

Aside from Eloy, the others were all in eighth through twelfth grade. Tall, strong, and hairy, they were signposts for how far Will had to go to grow up, and that made him feel like a little kid. Heck, next to them he *was* a little kid. Even the eighth graders seemed more filled out than he was.

Joining the group of twenty or so older guys, it was kind of nice to have Eloy with him.

Will set down his bag in an empty cubby near the door, Eloy in the one next to his, and he started to change as fast as he could, not wanting his bony butt hanging out in front of these guys any longer than necessary. So it was inconvenient that Trey noticed Will before he'd pulled up his gym shorts, standing there in only a T-shirt and boxer briefs.

"Hey, it's the Bug Buddies," Trey called. Trey, Kaleb, and Mikiah were the eighth graders on the team, so they absolutely knew about the stinkbug in the middle-school library, but the "bug buddies" comment made Will wonder what version they'd heard, reminding Will of how Hollie had talked about it at home.

"I heard about that," Max Henderson said. Max was a senior, and last year he'd taken down another wrestler in under forty-five seconds. It was such a good pin, even his opponent's teammates had congratulated him. Will wasn't sure how he felt about being known as a "bug buddy" by a guy like Max.

"Skin check!" someone shouted.

"Yeah, check for bugs!"

Trey grabbed Will in a loose headlock while Mikiah pretended to inspect Will, and Kaleb asked Eloy if he'd wrestled before and explained about skin checks. They were mandatory at every match, since wrestlers were constantly in physical contact with each other. Communicable skin diseases such as impetigo and ringworm were as yucky as they sounded and the reason mats were cleaned with a special disinfectant daily.

Will was pretty sure the guys were laughing *with* him, not *at* him, but he wasn't sure enough to know how to act. It didn't help that his butt was hanging out in his briefs just like he'd *not* wanted to happen his first day. After practice they'd all strip to only their skivvies for weigh-in, but Will had hoped they'd see that he knew what he was doing on the mats first.

"Find any bugs?" Max asked Mikiah, his tone making it clear he was only playing.

It was cool that someone like him would even notice Will, let alone joke with him, and the tightness in Will's gut loosened. He knew wrestlers. They were good guys, and he was one of them.

"No bugs," Mikiah announced.

"He's pretty stinky, though," Trey said, releasing Will with a grin.

"Worse than a protein-bar fart?" Kaleb asked. Everyone shuddered and groaned at the thought. Protein bars were a good way to build and maintain muscle mass without a lot of extra calories, but they caused farts that were basically weapons of mass destruction.

"Bugs are good for protein, too," Eloy said.

A chorus of "Eww!" "No way!" and "Bug eaters!" filled the air, along with a bunch of laughs.

Will had been worried, but now he channeled his inner Simon or something, because he jumped onto a bench and cocked his arms in a classic double-biceps pose. "I am Bug Boy! You want guns like these?" He flexed to show off the near-total absence of definition. "You've got to earn 'em."

The team's hoots rose out of the sweaty-feet funk of the locker room like the foot-stamping approval of a stadium of spectators. When a bunch of the guys struck their own far-more-impressive poses, Will was too busy grinning to feel intimidated.

Until Coach Van Beek shouted from the doorway, "You doing your hair in there? Get your butts out here."

Eloy, already stinky in the same shorts and tee he'd worn for P.E., walked beside Will. "When you talked about the wrestling team, I thought . . ." Eloy looked around at the guys, every single one taller than him. "Are we the only ones from our grade?"

Will might be new to this team, but Eloy was new, period, and Will didn't want him to be scared off. Though wrestling was popular in Minnesota, it was a tough sport. As guys got older and training and matches got more intense, many quit. Most teams only had two or three guys per grade and sometimes zero. The important thing wasn't necessarily the grade but one's weight.

"It can look a little intimidating," Will said, "but we wrestle by weight classes, so you'd never face someone like that." He tipped his head toward Randy Henderson, another senior and Max's cousin. Randy wrestled at 195, the heaviest weight class and twice as heavy as Will himself. Randy was seeded number one at tournaments a lot. Getting taken down by a guy like him had to be like getting hit by a train. Will swallowed. Holy cow, these guys were all so big.

With the team gathered, Coach Van Beek said, "You know what these first two weeks are about."

Conditioning, Will thought.

"Conditioning," Coach said. "All it takes to be a decent wrestler is to not quit." He looked at the other coaches: Will's science teacher, Mr. Taylor, and Mr. Jensen, whose three sons had all wrestled. "We're going to make you want to quit, and that's good. If you don't want to quit at least three times a week, you're not pushing yourself hard enough. Work through your point of failure. Be the one who makes the *other* guy quit. That's how you defeat opponents: You don't stop."

One thing Will knew he could do was not quit, and the other guys didn't look as if they *had* a point of failure. Even Eloy seemed ready. He stared at Coach as if he was trying to memorize every word.

Practice started with warm-up laps: forward run, backward run, lunges, forward roll, and cartwheels—genuinely pitiful cartwheels that would shame a kindergartner. The team was lucky they got to use the smaller gym all winter, separate from the main one. About the size of a basketball court with no sidelines, the floor was covered with thick maroon wrestling mats they were able to leave down all season and not have to roll out and put away for every practice.

They would practice five days a week now, then have a meet once a week and an all-day tournament most Saturdays, from mid-November through February. The work was tough and got to be a grind, but Will loved it. Everyone who stuck with wrestling had to love it. Maybe that meant they were all a little crazy, but at least they were in the right place for it. Because the gym was relatively small and used as a practice space by different teams, the walls were padded with maroon panels, too, about to the height of a door, so guys could bounce off them as they rounded corners or did sprints.

A padded room for the crazy people.

They wouldn't do any real sparring until they got through the first few days of soreness, so after stretching and strength training, Coach had them practice some basic breakdowns and escapes from the referee's starting position, keeping things low to the ground for now so no one would take a high fall before their bodies were ready.

Will and Eloy were paired up, but Eloy paused to watch the other guys for a few minutes.

The referee's starting position was one of the most basic elements of wrestling, executed many times during each match, thousands of times during a season. The bottom person got on his hands and knees, then sat back on his ankles. The top person wrapped him from behind, one knee up beside the other guy, one knee down behind him, an arm around his waist, a hand on his elbow, and his chin on the other guy's back. It didn't mean he had the advantage, but the top wrestler basically covered the bottom one with his body.

Will had been around wrestling too long to think anything about it anymore, but he knew what some people said.

"If you think it's gay, you should leave now," Will told Eloy. The team deserved respect, especially from its wrestlers.

"Huh?" Eloy blinked, then squinted at Will. "I'm watching to learn the moves. Today's my first day, remember?"

"Oh." Will's neck got hot.

"You're kind of touchy, aren't you?"

"Me?" Will wasn't the touchy one; that was Darryl. Will was the low-key guy who kept Darryl and/or Simon from getting out of hand. Too startled by the description to care about his tone, Will grumped, "Just get down, and I'll show you this one."

Coach Jensen came over for a few minutes and talked Eloy through the basic setups, the pros and cons of top and bottom, how to score points by breaking down an opponent from the top to move into a pinning combination or by escaping from the bottom to move into a reversal. Being Eloy's crash-test dummy should have made the exercise slow for Will, but it gave him time to think.

He *wasn't* touchy, but things *had* been out of whack since Eloy entered the picture.

Will's frustration made him too aggressive about the next practice breakdown. In seconds, he grabbed Eloy's ankle, lifted it as high as possible, then half stood to put his chest on Eloy's back and drive him forward. Eloy belly flopped onto the mat, hard.

"*¡Maldita sea!*" Eloy grunted.

Will snapped back onto his knees, giving Eloy space. That had been an uncool move. Sure, the guy was going to have to learn to take a face-plant—it happened to all of them—but not on his first day ever. "Sorry. That was rough."

Eloy pushed onto his elbows. "It wouldn't be so bad if the mat didn't reek."

New sweat, old sweat, feet, and disinfectant. The smells were like a third opponent on the mat, silent but deadly.

Will thought of a joke about what else was silent and deadly, when it hit him: Eloy had grunted and said something in Spanish, something in Spanish that Will suspected was of a very specific variety.

He plopped down onto Eloy, squishing him flat on his belly again, and demanded, "What did you say?"

ELOY DIDN'T KNOW TYPICAL WRESTLING MOVES, BUT HE
was strong and not happy to be nose-deep in the mat again.
He lifted his chest and twisted his shoulders, hard, butting
Will's chest and tipping him to the side. Eloy kept the turn
going, making Will sprawl, while Eloy pushed to his feet. Will
scrambled up, too, and grabbed Eloy's arm to pull him close.

"What's your problem?" Eloy said, too loudly.

"Shh! The coaches will hear."

Eloy pulled away, arms crossed.

"You said something in Spanish," Will whispered.

"So?" Eloy's jaw got all square, like he was clenching his
teeth.

Will peered at him. Eloy thought *Will* was touchy? "It
was a curse word, wasn't it?"

Eloy's cheeks darkened.

"It was!" Will barely stopped himself from jumping around. He clapped an arm over Eloy's shoulders and
crowed quietly, "You found the loophole!"

Eloy stared at him, waiting.

Will crowded in, whispering again, though it wasn't likely they'd be heard over the exertions of the other guys still practicing. "The coaches don't allow cursing, but you just did, and *no one knew.*" The significance of this blew Will's mind. "You've got to teach me."

"I'm not teaching you Spanish curses." Eloy sounded as if he meant it, but he had to bite his cheek to keep from smiling.

"You're not fooling anyone," Will said.

"No one knew I cursed because no one but you heard me. If my mom found out I was teaching my friends how to curse . . ." He paled in a way Will understood. Sure, Mom loved him and all, but that didn't mean she couldn't be scary when she was ticked. "Besides, in my house, they're not *Spanish* curses, just curses. If she heard me, Mom would put these guys to shame."

"My dad told me to wash my mouth out with soap yesterday."

Eloy's eyes went wide. "For real?"

"He didn't mean it. I don't think." Will was pretty sure anyway.

Thinking about Spanish and curses made Will think of another question he'd wanted to ask about but felt weird to. "So, uh, what about . . ." He adjusted a kneepad. Then the other one.

"What about what?" Eloy finally asked.

Will cleared his throat. *"Cholo?"*

Eloy rolled his eyes. "It doesn't mean anything."

Will doubted that. It definitely meant something when Darryl said it.

Eloy must have sensed Will's skepticism, because he added, "I mean, it's not a curse word."

Did that mean Darryl hadn't actually said anything racist? That didn't seem right, but Will couldn't explain why until Eloy, studying Will's face, said, "But then, neither is 'the Mexican.'"

Will got what Eloy meant. Darryl *thought* the word was a curse—and worse—so it was. Will sighed.

"Hey," Coach Van Beek snapped from right behind them, making them jump. "You planning world peace over here?"

Will and Eloy looked at each other. "Uh . . ."

"Then hit the mat."

He pointed down, and they dropped.

While Coach talked Eloy through another way to break down Will by grabbing his far foot and far knee, Will recalled Eloy saying, ". . . teaching my friends . . ." But whatever question Will might have had about the "friend" part flew away when his knees were pulled out from under him.

After practice, it was time to weigh in.

They'd weigh in every day so the coaches could be sure

all the weight classes were covered and the guys could keep track of progress as they tried to add or drop weight.

Weigh-ins were done in their skivvies, and half the guys had already stripped before the digital scale was tapped awake.

Eloy looked freaked.

Will was used to stripping down in front of strangers—refs did a weigh-in at every match, and showers were mandatory after every practice and competition—but he was kind of freaked this time, too.

Compared to guys like Max and Randy, Will felt like a kindergartner. At least he wasn't the only one. Eventually, this would be normal for him and Eloy. For now, they'd just have to gut it out. He offered Eloy a what-can-ya-do shrug in moral support.

Will's sweat-soaked T-shirt had cooled down and felt like slime sliding over his skin as he pulled it off. Eloy took an audible breath and followed suit.

Eloy had proved himself pretty strong during practice, and the guy already had muscle definition, especially in his shoulders but even a bit in his chest and legs. Will wasn't a wimp, but his height made him look stringy.

It was worse when they got onto the scale. They were both just below one hundred pounds.

Which meant they were in the same weight class.

Will told himself not to worry. He had years of wrestling

experience to Eloy's none. And because of that experience, Coach would wrestle Will on varsity and Eloy on JV. But Eloy had fast reflexes and a quick mind and muscle definition—and Will couldn't help but wonder how long his solo turn at seventh-grade varsity status would last.

THE NEXT MORNING, ELOY WAS AT WILL'S LOCKER FIRST
thing. "This isn't a joke, right?"

"Huh?"

Eloy glared down the hall at the yellow caution tape
strung across the library doors. "The grasshoppers. When I
asked my dad . . ."

Crap. His dad must have said no. After the deal Will had
made with Eloy about wrestling, and how much worse that
made things look to Darryl . . .

Will's locker squealed as he jerked it open.

"He's really excited," Eloy said, not sounding excited
himself.

"He's in?"

"For now."

"What's your problem?" Will didn't get why Eloy seemed
mad. Will had only asked for help. Eloy didn't have to agree.

"He's excited," Eloy said again. "He likes to share things
about where he's from. I just . . . It can't be a joke, okay?"

The spines of the books Will had wedged into his locker yesterday were twisted, and they bulged in a way that looked painful. His notebooks were in worse shape, with pages wrinkled and torn. A pen must have busted, too, because blue-black ink stained the edges of the notebook paper.

Will would never make fun of Eloy's dad—that was crazy—and part of him thought he should be mad at Eloy for thinking it. But the grasshoppers *were* for a joke—that was the whole point. It wasn't like they were really for food.

"No one will eat them if I don't make it funny," Will said. "They're *bugs*."

"There's a difference between being funny and being a joke."

Considering how recently Will had learned that personally, when he came to school thinking he'd be laughed at and instead was laughed with . . . "You don't have to worry about me," he said. And he meant it.

Eloy let out one of those cheek-puffing sighs that seemed like a cross between giving in and giving up. Now that he'd asked his dad, Eloy was clearly committed whether he liked it or not. Will was starting to feel the same way.

"Wait. Your dad can cook, right?"

Eloy rolled his eyes. "I wouldn't have agreed to ask him if he couldn't."

"Yeah, well, my dad says he can cook, too, but you only eat his chili if you want to shoot flames out of your butt."

That cracked up Eloy, though at Will's grumpy expression, he tried to hold it back. "Your butt's shot flames?"

"See, this is when one of those Spanish curses would come in handy."

"Hmm, how about *trasero en llamas*?"

"Ooo, what's that mean?"

"'Flaming butt of doom.'"

Will popped Eloy in the arm, but it only made him laugh.

"It'll be fine," Eloy said. "My dad owns a restaurant."

"Cool." The plan had a fifty-fifty shot if the grasshoppers were actually almost edible. "Wait. You moved here from Rochester, right?"

"Yeah. That's where the restaurant is, but the Mayo Clinic center in Owatonna offered Mom a really good job, and Dodge Center's kind of in the middle."

As if Will cared about any of that. The thought that had exploded in his head was a thousand times more important than freaking geography. "Does your dad own a Mexican restaurant?"

"Are you being totally racist?"

"What? No! You said he's from Mexico!"

Eloy laughed in Will's face. "Dude. I'm just busting on you. Yes, Dad serves Mexican and other Latin American food. El Corazón, out by the—"

"By the movie theater!" Will shouted. "That's my favorite place!" He wished Rochester were closer so they could eat there all the time, but he always picked it first for his birthday and stuff like that. He popped Eloy's arm harder this time. "Why didn't you tell me sooner?!"

"Quit hitting me, dork-face."

"Tell me you can get me food. Omigosh, I'd eat those tamales every day."

"I *am* getting you food, remember?"

"The chalupines don't count." Though if they tasted as good as everything else Mr. Herrera made, then maybe they did.

"What did you call them?"

"I looked them up. That's their name." Duh.

Eloy laughed hard enough that some snot bubbled out of his nose.

"Do you need to roll around on the floor, too?" Will grumbled.

"*Chapulines,* not chalupines. *Chap*-oo-*leen*-ess," Eloy said, all fancy-Spanish-like.

"Whatever. I don't speak Spanish."

"I know," Eloy said. "I'm in Spanish class with you."

Will couldn't stop himself from snorting. That was a good one.

"Wait," he said. "El Corazón is Darryl's favorite place, too. You'll totally be best friends when he finds out."

"Why would I want to be friends with him?"

From close behind them, very close, Darryl said, "You gonna let him talk about me like that?"

THE LOCKERS WERE TALL ENOUGH THAT IF THEY DIDN'T have shelves, Will could have fit inside.

Instead, he stood with his open door a thin shield between Darryl and Eloy, with himself in the middle.

This would have been another really good time for one of those Spanish curse words Eloy wouldn't teach him yet.

"No," he said to Darryl, meaning it. "Jeez, Eloy."

Why wouldn't Eloy want to be friends with Darryl? Wasn't it enough that Darryl was Will's friend?

But as soon as he had the thought, Will realized how stupid it was.

If the situation were reversed, and Eloy had called Darryl some name, Darryl would never laugh it off and become friends with him as if it had never happened. Had Will really thought Eloy would? Especially when Darryl hadn't simply called Eloy "some name"; he'd given him crap about who he *was*. Will, Darryl, and Simon called one another dorks and jerks and idiots all the time, but it wasn't the same, and Will knew it.

"Why are you hanging out with him anyway?" Darryl said to Will.

Will's space in the middle seemed to shrink in half. Why wasn't Eloy leaving? Will would have by now and not cared what it looked like. "He joined wrestling. He's got a lot to learn."

Darryl kicked at a locker—not hard, just to be doing something and not looking at them. "So you're best friends now?" Before Will could deny it, Darryl added, mumbling to his foot, "I say one thing, and you freak out."

Will glanced at Eloy, eyes wide. What Darryl had just said was about as close to an apology as he would give, and Will hadn't expected it at all. But Eloy didn't get it—he had an eyebrow cocked and wore a dubious look—and Will sighed. Even if Will knew what a big deal it was for Darryl to acknowledge that maybe he'd said something uncool, it wasn't enough, because Eloy didn't know, and he was the one who mattered in this case.

"So what were you talking about?" Darryl asked.

It took Will only a few seconds to backtrack and remember they were talking about Eloy's dad and El Corazón just before Darryl showed up. But those few seconds were too long for Darryl.

"Whatever," he said, acting as if it didn't matter and giving the locker one last kick. "If I really cared, Simon would spill."

"Hey!" Simon complained from behind a locker door that wasn't his. "You didn't have to out me like that."

"But I don't," Darryl continued. When he turned to go, his shoulder bumped Will's chest, and Will wanted to yield but had no room, since his back was already half in his locker.

After seven years of being friends with the guy, Will knew when Darryl's feelings were hurt. On a normal day, Will might have pulled him aside to say he was sorry, but Will wasn't sure what, if anything, he was supposed to be sorry for. So Darryl walked away alone.

"Where's he going?" Simon asked. "His locker's right here."

They all watched as Darryl ignored the caution tape across the library doors, jerked one open, and walked inside.

"Whoa," Simon said.

The library wasn't exactly surrounded with crime scene tape, but still. The move was too hard-core to think Darryl was hiding out from anyone, especially his two best friends.

"Well, maybe that will calm down Mr. Grumpypants," Simon said.

"Don't call him that." Will darted a glance at Eloy.

"Fine, Mr. Grumpypants," Simon said, then held up his phone while he started googling. "How do you spell *chapulines*?"

Will grabbed for the phone, but Simon played keep-away, practically waving it—and its Google search—in the faces of everyone in the hallway.

"It won't be funny if everyone knows what's coming," Will whisper-shouted.

That got Simon's attention. He tucked the phone into his jeans, then crossed his arms. "I shouldn't have to sneak around to find out what you're up to."

"'Spy' is the word you're looking for," Will grumped.

"It wasn't like we were hiding," Eloy said, gesturing down the wide hallway.

Simon squinted at Eloy. "What Darryl said the other day wasn't cool, but that doesn't mean you and me are friends yet."

Will felt Eloy look at him, but Will was kind of in shock. Simon being serious was like a meteor shower. It happened, but not often.

"Things have been out of whack ever since you entered the picture," Simon added.

"I've been here two months," Eloy said, though all three knew Simon meant since what had happened in the library. "Besides, you didn't mind it yesterday when you were getting a bunch of attention."

"But what have you done for me lately?" Simon managed a little smirk to make it a joke, but the smile came too slowly and went too fast.

Eloy rolled his eyes. "I'll see you at practice," he said to Will, even though they'd "see" each other in four classes first.

Simon watched him walk to his locker. "So, what's this new plan?"

"Don't. Tell. Anyone." Will wasn't sure it was a good idea, but it would be a terrible idea if people found out about it first.

"I don't have anything *to* tell," Simon grumbled. "I can't believe *he* knows but *I* don't."

"What's that supposed to mean?" Will snapped, Simon's tone making him remember the way Darryl had said "*cholo*" and "the Mexican."

"He just moved here," Simon argued. "I've known you since you were *born*."

Relief made Will snicker. "I've known you that long, too, Mr. Sure-I-Can-Keep-a-Secret."

"It happened one time," Simon moaned.

"The Saran Wrap incident. The Ping-Pong incident. And don't even get me started on the noodle incident."

"The noodle incident!" Simon sighed. "Ah, good times."

Will laughed, then quickly explained about getting the class to eat grasshoppers and how Eloy's dad was going to help. In general, Simon was excited by a lot of things, but his reaction to Will's plan confirmed that Will was about to make history. Simon was more than excited. He was awed.

It was almost intimidating.

"I'm not sure I can pull it off," Will admitted.

"Don't worry," Simon said, pretty much guaranteeing

that Will would worry. There were a lot of things to worry about lately.

"We have to figure out something about Darryl." Will didn't want Darryl to feel left out, but he didn't want him to ruin things, either.

"He'll cool down."

It was somewhat routine: Wait for Darryl to cool down, and act as if nothing had happened. But the thought didn't quite reassure Will this time.

The warning bell rang, and Eloy walked by with Cristian on their way to social studies.

Will looked away and grabbed his books, reminding himself not to worry. Everything would be fine.

THE FIRST THREE DAYS OF WRESTLING PRACTICE KICKED
Will's butt.

He loved it.

Each ache and pain said, "You did the work. You earned me." Will liked that feeling, and Eloy seemed to, too. It felt good to work hard with like-minded people who shared the same goal of squishing another guy flat.

By Saturday and their first half-day practice, Will was tired and sore and totally pumped. Coach made the day a technique clinic, moving them through a broad range of key wrestling moves, explaining the *why* of every move. Something as simple as one's stance could give a smaller wrestler an advantage over a bigger but less experienced one, good posture providing balance and the ability to move quickly in any direction. The coaches covered every major body part. Quick and efficient feet to move all over the mat. Knees kept bent in a Z for flexibility and strength. Hips the core of using the upper and lower body together in connected, fluid moves. Arms critical to every takedown and counterattack. Even the head a strong resource to hold positions or break out of them.

And that was only half the awesomeness of the day. Since the point was to practice slowly, watching body position and thinking through how moves could flow into one another, the coaches disregarded weight while pairing the guys. They changed up practice partners throughout the day, so Will got to know everyone a little better. Facing off with big guys like Max and Randy was scary no matter how slowly they went, but both were totally cool. Max joked around about Bug Boy, and Randy was mellow, explaining where he thought Will could adjust for better positioning. Will relaxed in no time, beginning to feel like a real part of the team. He noticed that Eloy seemed to be doing OK, too.

Afterward, Coach Van Beek pulled Will aside and said he had a good technical foundation and was looking forward to seeing him grow. Will bit his lip to keep from grinning like a loon and planned to beg Mom to buy a giant box of protein bars so he could add some muscle and weight. Coach meant "see Will grow" as a wrestler, but Will wanted to grow, period.

Eloy pulled Will aside, too, and invited him to his house on Sunday.

"Uhh." They hadn't really talked until this week, and now they were going to each other's houses?

But then Eloy added, "Come on. We can practice the wrestling moves some more, and you can meet my dad."

That made Will's heart speed up and his mouth water. "Will he cook something?"

"You're obsessed."

"I'm focused."

"Is that a yes, then?"

It didn't seem right to agree solely in the hope of being fed, so Will thought about putting him off by saying he was grounded, even though he knew Mom would let him go because of wrestling . . . and probably because of Eloy.

But then he saw the yellow cover of the *Wrestling for Dummies* book in Eloy's bag. The guy hadn't even thought of joining the team until Wednesday. Eloy was committed, that was for sure, and Will *had* promised to help him learn.

Will told him to text the address.

After that, Will was more than ready to get home. The practice may have been "slow," but that made it harder in some ways, because they had to control their movements more and hold positions longer. Will showered in the locker room like everyone else, but at home he could stand under extra-hot water until it ran out.

Dad was driving a train, so Will texted him that practice was over so he could call if he got a break. Engineers weren't allowed to use their phones while driving, but since the trains frequently were stopped for long stretches, he could sometimes check in for a few minutes. Will's dad had wrestled, too, so it was cool to talk with him and break down some of the techniques Will was working on. But Dad's being gone meant it was just Will and "the girls" all weekend, which was the kind of thing Dad could say but Mom and Hollie didn't let Will get away with for some reason.

When Will walked in, Hollie was at the coffee table decorating a poster board with glitter, gunking up the living room with red and silver sparkles. He knew from experience that they would end up in his clothes and hair no matter how much distance he kept from them, and it was always bad when the guys spotted glitter he'd missed.

"You've got a room," he told her.

"Your face needs bedazzling," she said. "Not that it would make a difference."

"Mom," Will complained.

"The vacuum is already out," Mom said. As if that helped.

Will huffed, because Hollie always got her way, then thumped his sweaty gear onto the washer. He washed his stuff every day to prevent skin infections, but with Sunday off tomorrow, he went ahead and did an extra clean, including getting everything together to wash his gym bag, plus his wrestling shoes in a pillowcase. Mom kept antibacterial wipes in the small alcove for him so he could wipe down his headgear and kneepads, too. He wondered if anyone had told Eloy about preventing the skin stuff, and that made him remember Eloy's gear—because he had some. He must have gone to the sports store in Rochester right after their first practice on Wednesday. And it wasn't as if wrestling shoes, headgear, and kneepads were cheap. Eloy was seriously committed.

The small laundry area filled with the stink of Will's clothes.

He remembered making the deal to help Eloy practice, thinking it wasn't a big deal, because Eloy would quit after the first practice. Though he hadn't been Will's teammate at the time, it now felt disloyal to have had that thought about someone who had proved himself to be so determined.

When the doorbell rang, he flinched.

"Will you get that, Will?" Mom called.

On his way to the door, he passed the kitchen and took a deep sniff of the smells of ground beef and taco mix in the air. It was really early for dinner, but Mom stirred the sizzling meat and had already covered the counters with chopped lettuce, shredded cheese, and open containers of sour cream and salsa. Hard shells from the taco kit were on a baking pan ready to go into the oven. "You're cooking?"

Mom gave him a look.

"You know what I mean."

She smiled. "Hollie and I ran a bunch of errands and didn't have lunch. I figured you'd be hungry, too."

He grunted because, yes, he was always hungry.

"Use your words, fuzz-butt," Hollie said.

Will growled as he passed her and the glitter island she'd made in the living room.

"Nice." She blew a puff of silver glitter at him.

"Mom!" he yelled, but then whoever was at the door knocked.

Will opened it to a UPS guy.

And a box marked Live Crickets.

"DELIVERY FOR WILL NOLAN," THE UPS GUY SAID.

"Uh," Will said.

Bigger than a winter-boot shoe box, the cardboard had mesh openings on the sides for air flow and was stamped with bright red text about dry feed and clean water. Arrows pointed THIS WAY UP next to FRAGILE repeated three times in a row. And in all caps: LIVE CRICKETS.

"Uh," Will said again.

The UPS guy winked. "I bet these are for you. An adult is supposed to sign, but you give me your John Hancock, and we'll call it even."

Will took the plastic stylus and signed his name, but when the box was handed over, Will just stood there, door open, holding it. A box of live crickets.

"Uh."

"Close the door," Hollie said. "It's freezing out."

It was. It was the kind of cold that meant it was even

too cold to snow. Not that anyone expected real, stick-around snow this early in November. Or crickets. Nobody expected crickets in November, either. They were summer-night bugs, so why the heck was he holding a large box of them?

"What are you doing?" Hollie snapped, approaching to slam the door with a *bang* loud enough to scare a few crickets. He could tell, because they chirped.

Hollie screamed.

And flailed, smacking the box out of his hands.

It landed THIS WAY UP, which was good, but a lot of crickets sprang at the mesh openings. A lot.

"What's going on?" Mom asked. The stove clicked as she turned it off.

Hollie stepped back and bumped into the coffee table, knocking off her half-finished poster and a large shaker of red glitter. "It's a box of bugs!" She shuddered in a wiggle dance that smeared glue onto the carpet and floated glitter into the air.

"What?" Mom said. "But . . . what?"

Will stared down at the large box at his feet by the door. It seemed wrong to leave the creatures toppled there.

He picked them up. He walked to the sofa and sat down with the box on his lap. A large box. A large box of a lot of live crickets.

"Get them out of here," Hollie said, backing away, red

glitter streaming from beneath her feet. It was kind of mesmerizing, actually. Then the box moved.

Instinctively, Will pushed it away. It slid down his shins, hooked at his feet, and tilted. On its side was a THIS WAY UP in red. He picked up the box and put it beside him on the couch.

"Who on earth sent them?" Mom asked.

"Oh," Hollie said, "we all know which of Will's bone-headed friends would think this is funny." She glared at Will like it was his fault Simon had pranked him.

Will blankly read off the return label indicating that the crickets had come from a company called JurassiPets. He guessed the actual sender would likely be listed on a statement inside, but he was in no hurry to open the box.

"You just *had* to eat that stupid stinkbug, didn't you?"

"We don't *know* it's from him," Will said, defending his friend even though he one hundred percent knew it was from Simon. His dad had left Simon's mom and taken off to Arizona with a girlfriend, leaving Simon behind with a credit card to make up for not calling much or ever visiting. So Simon made a point of only using the card for ridiculous stuff like this.

Will shifted the box and peered through a mesh opening on the side. Packing material shaped like the bottom half of an egg carton was layered inside to create pods of space for the crickets to gather in. But some clung to the mesh. Others walked around. Between the jostling of travel and the house's warmth, the crickets were waking up. Except the box, like, *vibrated*. The crickets weren't "waking up"; they were *awake*. What he guessed might be a thousand crickets were *wide* awake.

"I could strangle that kid," Mom said with feeling. "What could Simon possibly think you would do with them?"

"Anybody could have sent them," Will argued. "I *am* Bug Boy now." The return label only had the company name. "Maybe there's a note inside."

"Don't you dare open that box!" Hollie said.

Mom sighed. "I'll call Renée. She can pick up the crickets and have a long, *long* talk with Simon."

Will's mom calling Simon's mom? That would be even more of a disaster than Simon sending the crickets in the first place! In panic, Will blurted, "Maybe Mr. Herrera can take them?"

"Why in the world would Mr. Herrera want them?" Mom asked.

Will hadn't told her about the science presentation they'd been assigned. He hadn't wanted to risk her saying no to it. But what the heck was he supposed to do with a thousand crickets?

"He . . . he has a restaurant."

"I know, but he's not going to—"

"You do? How did you know that?" Will had only found out this week that Eloy's dad owned El Corazón.

"His daughter is in my class," Mom said. "I recognized

him from El Corazón, and I doubt very much he needs *crickets* for his restaurant."

"Uh, Eloy said that where his dad's from, they eat grasshoppers, and I've heard about stuff like cricket tacos." While he was researching the *chapulines*, not that he would explain that part.

"You're not putting crickets on our tacos," Hollie said at the same time Mom said, "The man's not going to serve bugs to his customers."

"They're supposed to be really good," Will argued. *He* didn't want to eat a giant box of crickets, but in theory, they were fine. Like, for other people.

"I'll drive you to those woods by the stream," Mom said. "You can release them, and—"

"And they'll die," Will said. It was too cold out. They might be only crickets, but he didn't want a thousand of them to die for no reason. "At least let me ask Mr. Herrera."

Mom sighed, then threw up her hands. "I guess. If he wants them, I'll drive you over."

"Can you at least put them in the garage for now?" Hollie pleaded. Then she noticed the spilled glitter, smeared glue, and bent poster board—her project in ruins. "I will feed you to those crickets, Will!"

Hollie pulled off her sticky socks and rubbed at glue on the carpet while Mom darted to the kitchen for a wet towel. Will left the box on the sofa and made a fast exit from the cleaning crew, calling, "I need my phone to call Eloy." He knew where Mom kept it when he was grounded from using it.

Her underwear drawer.

Mom was crazy smart, because no way Will went in there unless he had to. This was a desperate time, but after he got the phone, he hesitated. It was one thing to ask a guy to help make a few edible grasshoppers for school. What would he think about something like this?

Will procrastinated by catching up on the texts he'd missed since Tuesday morning. Simon had sent dozens, even after he knew Will didn't have his phone anymore, like little joke land mines waiting for him.

Darryl had sent one.

From Tuesday afternoon, it said only, *Dude.* Will wasn't sure how to read it. Was it *Dude, I'm so ticked at you.* Or *Dude, are we cool?* Or even *Dude, you ate a stinkbug!*

A lot had happened since then, but Will wanted to think he and Darryl were still cool. So he wrote back, "Covert op. Phone back in drawer soon. Just saying hey."

Then he took a deep breath and called Eloy.

"Hey," Eloy answered.

"Hey," Will said. Then didn't say anything else. How did a person start a conversation to pawn off a thousand crickets onto someone else? He kind of worried it wasn't fair to even try.

"We still on for tomorrow?" Eloy asked.

"What? Oh, yeah." Will said, remembering their extra practice. He definitely had other things than wrestling on his mind right now.

"So what's going on?" Eloy asked.

Will heaved a sigh. "Someone sent me a box of crickets. Live ones. A lot of them."

"And by someone, you mean Simon?"

"Well," Will huffed, "I don't know for *sure*."

"Uh-huh," Eloy said, clearly not believing him.

Will totally knew for sure.

"And when you say 'a lot,'" Eloy said, "are we talking, like, a hundred?"

"Uh." Will cleared his throat. "I mean, if I had to guess . . . a thousand?"

Eloy snorted a laugh. "It would have been funnier if he'd sent them to school, but the principal probably wouldn't have actually passed them on to you or anything."

Will hadn't even thought of that, but Eloy was right. How funny was a prank if no one saw it?

"What did he say when you called him on it?" Eloy asked.

"I haven't yet. My mom wants to call his mom."

"Oh crap."

"I know! I hoped maybe you could help me?" The back of his neck heated with more than embarrassment as he thought to himself, *Help me*, again.

"How?"

"I thought maybe your dad might want them? For the restaurant?"

Eloy paused. "You know your mom's probably going to call his mom anyway, right?"

Did Will know that? He slumped. Of course he did. Heck, she might even be on the phone with her already. As soon as Will hung up, he'd have to text Simon a warning. Though that was more than Simon had done for Will before sending him *a thousand crickets*, the bonehead.

"Let me see what Dad says," Eloy sighed.

Will heard Eloy walking to another room, then talking in Spanish with his dad for what seemed like forever. What the heck would Mr. Herrera think of Will after this? They hadn't even met yet, and now this. Will thought he might have to strangle Simon, too.

Finally, Eloy came back on. "He said where are they from?"

He'd clearly said a lot more than that, which didn't bode well. "JurassiPets?"

Will could practically hear Eloy wince over the phone. "So they weren't raised for human consumption, which means Dad can't serve them. But I'm sure a pet store will take them."

Dodge Center didn't have a pet store. They'd have to go all the way out to Owatonna or Rochester, which no way

Mom would do for Simon's prank. Will had tried, but Simon was definitely getting in trouble for this one—not that Will was sure he minded.

"Or," Eloy said. "Do you know someone with animals?"

"Even if I knew someone who had a lizard, I doubt their mom would be any more excited about a box of a thousand crickets."

"No, like cows or pigs or something," Eloy explained. "Dad said they're good animal feed."

Animal feed! That was a great idea! They were in *Minnesota*. Everyone knew someone with cows. Though a cow trying to chase down a cricket . . . that had to be the funniest thing ever. Will could laugh simply imagining it.

"Just freeze them," Eloy added.

"What?"

"Dad said to freeze the crickets. Then whoever can add them to the feed whenever, and they'll still be fresh."

"Oh," Will said.

Freeze them. As in kill them. Kill a thousand crickets just because.

Yes, he had eaten a stinkbug and planned to eat a grasshopper and had read that crickets were great on tacos. But still.

"What's taking you so long?" Hollie demanded from the doorway, startling Will into dropping his phone onto Mom's underwear—ick. "You can help, too, you know."

"It's *your* glitter."

"And it's *your* bug-brained friend sending boxes of bugs that—"

"Hello?" Eloy's voice said from the drawer.

Will grabbed the phone. "Sorry. Gotta go. Thanks for helping." Though as he hung up, he wasn't sure Eloy's idea was help exactly.

He must have looked rattled, because Hollie asked, "What is it? You OK?"

"His dad said to freeze them," Will explained. "All of them."

"Oh," Hollie said.

Will put the phone back and slowly closed the drawer. "Some insects have their own antifreeze," he mumbled, a fact he'd learned while starting to pull stuff together for his presentation. Some winter days Will wished he had anti-freeze, too.

"Do crickets?" Hollie asked.

Will shook his head. He didn't think so.

After a while, Hollie leaned a little so their shoulders touched, and he let her. "I'm sorry, Will."

They went back to the living room and told Mom. Every-one looked at the box.

Crickets explored the dimensions of the mesh, crawled to their neighbors' pods and over one another's bodies, and clung to the "ceiling" like party animals.

"It's supposed to be in the thirties tonight," Mom said. "It'll be quick."

She was right. He could just put the box outside. It *was*

cold. But freezing? He wasn't sure. He didn't want the little critters to suffer any longer than they had to.

"I should take them out of the box."

"What? No!" Hollie protested.

"The cardboard and the cartons inside will insulate them some. If they cluster in the middle, it could take a long time before they . . ."

"Oh," Mom and Hollie said.

They stared at the box some more. It seemed to jiggle, though it might have been a trick of the light.

It was stupid to be upset. The crickets were raised to be lizard food or whatever. Will had killed plenty of bugs in his lifetime and had eaten a stinkbug (who, to be fair, had gotten its revenge) and was soon going to eat a grasshopper. This wasn't really any different.

Except it was.

"Okay," Will said. He had to do it fast. They were only crickets. It wasn't a big deal.

He set the box on the kitchen table. "I'll just get them out of the box and take the bag outside." He glanced at Hollie, and she reluctantly handed him the scissors she'd been using. Then she backed away to behind the sofa.

Will rolled his eyes and pointed at the openings in the side of the box. "They're enclosed in mesh, see? And it's not like crickets bite."

At the word *bite*, Hollie shuddered.

"I'll hold the box steady," Mom offered. "You don't want to cut through the mesh bag accidentally."

He definitely didn't want to do that and thought about asking her to do the honors. But he didn't want to be a coward.

While Mom held the box steady, Will used one blade of the scissors to poke carefully at the seams sealed with papery brown tape. It was the kind with threads in it to make it tougher, so after a while the only way to finish was for Will to slip his fingers beneath the edges and give a good yank.

He did. The tape ripped with a series of pops.

Then something else popped against the cardboard flaps.

And another something.

Then a whole bunch of somethings.

The crickets weren't in mesh after all.

And now they weren't in the box.

16

A CRICKET SMACKED HIS CHEEK.

Another landed on his head.

He yelped and batted it off.

One hit the kitchen floor.

Where it landed with other crickets.

Not that many. Fifteen? Twenty?

Then the box *moved*. Crickets jumped onto Will, and Will jumped away from the table, hitting it with his legs, jarring the box just enough to slide to the edge, tip, and fall. It landed on its side with a thud that jarred loose the egg crates, layers tipping out like a paper fan opening up.

A cricket could jump twenty to thirty times its body length, and these did.

A lot jumped for the nearest heat source, landing on the brick chimney with audible ticks. Others went in different directions.

An orchestra of crickets dove into Mom's messily knotted

hair as if it were good cover. Shrieking, she ripped out her hair tie and bent over, shaking her hair free and making crickets rain down.

Others launched themselves toward the living room and landed on the coffee table with poofs of glitter. Hollie screamed and ducked behind the couch. Crickets followed. Glitter streamed in the air behind them as they made landings. On Hollie.

In the kitchen, crickets sank into salsa and sour cream. A few must have made their way free—thin red and white lines trailed across the counter like muddy footprints.

Some crickets stayed near the box, shaking as if they were cold or scared, and secreted a brown liquid.

Will did a dance as crickets slid beneath his collar and crawled up his jeans. He flapped his shirt and kicked his legs. It didn't help to tell himself not to be freaked out because they were only crickets. They were a *lot* of crickets.

Spreading fast and far as they made their break for freedom.

Then they started chirping.

He'd read only males chirped, usually to get girls. But sometimes to establish territory. And there was a lot of new territory to lay claim to.

For a few seconds, Will, Mom, and Hollie stilled. Chirping echoed down the hallway, bounced around the kitchen, reverberated up the chimney. Though totally out of place, it was kind of wonderful. Like lying in a field as the sun set on a summer day. A very large field. Swarming with crickets.

"Open the door," Hollie said. "Make them go outside."

If Will opened the door, the crickets would only back away. It was November out there. Freezing. Crickets weren't stupid.

But it finally occurred to Will to get the box and its remaining inhabitants outside. He tilted the egg crates back in. A few crickets got squished. Guts smeared the sides.

Though he carried them to certain death, he handled the box as gently as he could.

The night was still. Stars spread a net across the clear sky.

Will walked the box to the middle of the yard, his socks crunching on brittle grass. His chilled clothes stiffened and crinkled like paper. A cricket fell from his shirt's hem. In the box, maybe a third of the crickets remained. They huddled in the corners; a few slid to the bottom. They were all going to die.

Will's fingers felt frozen to the cardboard, ready to break off like icicles. Air burned his lungs.

He set down the box. He didn't look inside again. He went back to the house.

Mom was vacuuming up crickets and glitter with the Dirt Devil. Hollie braved the couch to get her laptop and look up ways to catch the rest. A Google search became their checklist.

First and easiest: Set out strips of duct tape. Dad always joked that duct tape fixed everything, and here was another example.

Mom found a jar of molasses. Apparently, crickets' love for the thick brown goo was suicidal. Will and Hollie set out bowls with a layer of the water-thinned stuff in the bottom.

Last, Will raided the recycling bin for the plastic bottles of seltzer Mom liked and Hollie wouldn't drink because she had read that bubbles made you fart. They cut off the bottle tops, inverted them into the bottom half, sprinkled sugar inside, and set them out.

By the time they were done, a couple hundred corpses and not-quite corpses were piled around the three of them.

He was glad he hadn't been alone when the crickets escaped. Mom being so matter-of-fact about having to catch and clean up bugs kept him from losing it. She taught kindergarten, so she was used to snot and stickiness, but this was a whole new level of "ick." And Hollie, she'd been creeped out by the bugs from the beginning but had gutted it out to help him.

When Dad called to check in and heard what had happened, he asked if they wanted him to call his brother. Uncle Rick lived on a lake, which meant summer at his place was Mosquito City, so he always had exterminator-level bug spray on hand. But Mom didn't like the idea of using stuff like that in the house in winter, especially since Dad had already put up the shrink film to insulate the windows. They were just going to have to hope the traps kept working.

No one seemed to blame Will, but he did. Simon had sent him a box of bugs because he was Bug Boy. It wouldn't have been funny if he weren't.

But it wasn't funny, and Will should have just let Mom call Simon's mom rather than try to fix it himself. More importantly, he shouldn't have opened the box.

It had been reasonable to think they were in some kind of bag inside, hadn't it? He'd seen the mesh in the box's "windows." And how could the crickets have been piled in and stayed in the box long enough to close it without some kind of net? Not that it mattered anymore. A few hundred were outside, freezing. A few hundred more were trapped and dying. And it was likely that another few hundred were roaming the house, searching for hideouts.

If he had only *known* the crickets were coming. But what would he have done then, really?

All these dead crickets. Tomorrow the story might be funny. Most of a thousand crickets *had* escaped in his house.

But tonight he just couldn't see the humor.

17

THAT NIGHT, WILL CLIMBED INTO BED AND SHOOED CRICK-
ets from under the blankets. Chirps echoed in the house's
hollow places, reverberations off-tempo and alien.

Darkness made his ceiling seem farther away. He stared
at it a long time.

The next morning, Hollie held open a heavy-duty lawn
bag for Will to collect the dead crickets, even though he
told her she didn't have to. Every now and then a chirp
made her whip her head around to make sure no crickets
were dive-bombing her hair again, but she never dropped
the bag. It quickly filled with strips of cricket-covered
duct tape and cricket-filled plastic bottles. The molasses
traps were the toughest. He couldn't throw away the glass
bowls, but the sticky bugs wouldn't slide out. He had to
rinse them in the sink, then scoop out the cricket corpses.
Though they collected hundreds, Will suspected there
were still a lot of crickets hiding out in the house.

Remembering the ones outside, he took a Ziploc bag to collect them, the only crickets left that could be animal feed and not have died for nothing.

Frost grayed the ground. The box, bent and ripped, looked like an abandoned building. But it wasn't. Inside, crickets had clustered together in a last stand against the cold, but there were no survivors.

Will held one in his palm. It was less than an inch long and almost weightless. The exoskeleton was brittle; he wasn't sure if that was normal or because of the cold or maybe a little of both. Bits looking like fingernail clippings chipped off as he turned it. Its six legs were curled in, even the larger jumper legs pinched together under its belly. But it still had poking things on both ends, antennae on its head and three other things on its rear. He wasn't sure what they were. The insect was so compact, the brownish-gray color made it look kind of like a pebble. Except it was definitely a cricket. A dead one of many dead ones.

His shiver made his neck crack.

It was stupid to have brought a Ziploc outside to bag the crickets where it was freezing. He picked up the box of crickets and carried it into the house. Maybe a little part of him hoped the heat would wake a few, but they poured out into the plastic bag in a lumpy, dull-brown stream.

On their way to Eloy's, they swung by Diggy's house to drop off the insects for his show steer. Then Mom drove to the big new subdivision that had taken over some cornfields not far from school. Will wasn't convinced she knew where she was going.

"Uh, the address is Longspur Lane?"

Mom cut him one of *those* looks but spotted the house number she wanted and pulled in behind a beater truck that might once have been red but had faded almost to orange. But beside it was a new dark-blue SUV.

The house was two stories with stonework on the bottom half. The chimney puffed smoke into a cartoon-blue sky. Big, leafy ferns and other plants inside framed the large picture window. It was a really nice house. Much nicer than Will's. Eloy definitely wasn't poor.

Heat zipped from the back of Will's neck to the tips of his ears.

When had he decided Eloy was poor? More important, why? Now that Will thought about it, Eloy dressed like everyone else, had a phone, and had gotten all his wrestling stuff right away. The only difference was his skin color. But Will would never say things like Darryl had—not to mention, he'd eaten a freaking stinkbug for the guy!

The reminder didn't stop the twisting in his gut. His feet dragged as he followed Mom to the front door.

She didn't get a chance to knock. The door was heaved open by a little girl who lunged for Mom's legs, making Mom laugh as she squatted to return the hug. "Hi there, Elsi."

It was always a little weird to run into one of Mom's kindergarten students. Will thought his mom was cool and loved her and all that, but her students *loved*-loved her. Sometimes it felt a little competitive.

Mrs. Herrera was only seconds behind Elsi and said something in superfast Spanish like he'd only ever heard on TV. Even their Spanish teacher wasn't that fast.

"But it's Mrs. Nolan," the girl protested.

"I've told you a thousand times," Eloy's mom said in English that sounded like everyone else in Minnesota, "don't answer the door by yourself." Then she turned to them with a smile. "Hi, Tara. Will, it's nice to meet you. Come on in."

"You talk so good," Will blurted.

"Unlike you," Mom snapped.

His body basically burst into flames. "I meant, like, the Spanish and stuff."

"Duh, *menso*," said Eloy, who had joined the crowd at the door.

His mom cuffed the back of Eloy's head before turning back to Will. "I was born here and gravitate toward English like Eloy and the girls, so we keep up our Spanish by using it at home."

"It sounds awesome," Will said.

"For all you know, she said the alphabet," Eloy said, the smack talk earning a look from his mom just like the ones Will got from his own mom. "Sorry," Eloy muttered.

While the moms talked about pickup times and other mom stuff, Will glanced around the house, then squinted because something seemed off. Eloy's house looked a lot like Will's, though bigger and newer. Long, dark-blue couch and love seat. A coffee table made with wood that still had bark on it, something Dad would like. Thick, comfy carpet his toes could sink into. A pale stone fireplace. Bookshelves with a full set of Harry Potter books at eye level.

Will's gut coiled up again.

He hadn't known it until he saw it, but Will had expected Eloy's house to look Mexican, like his dad's restaurant or something. There *was* a colorful woven hanging on the wall, and on end tables and shelves some really neat carvings of funky animals painted in bright colors, neither of which looked like they were from around here. But basically Eloy's house was pretty ordinary. Why had Will assumed it wouldn't be? What kind of person did that make Will?

The icky feeling shifted to full-on pukiness.

"You okay?" Eloy asked.

Will tried to shrug off his thoughts. They were only stupid thoughts. He didn't mean them the way they sounded. Not meaning something in a mean way meant it wasn't mean, right? Especially if you only think it and don't say it?

"So what did you end up doing with the crickets?" Eloy asked.

"We gave the ones that were left to a guy who shows steers," Will said, only half listening to himself because the mention of crickets reminded Will of grasshoppers, reminding him that Mrs. Herrera probably knew about them by now—and Will's mom didn't.

"The ones that were left?" Eloy said, confused, but Will had already dashed to the kitchen, where the moms had moved, praying hard he wasn't too late.

Luckily, Mom was oohing over some green pottery Mrs. Herrera said was made near where her husband grew up. One vase was really cool with three lizards coiled around like they were circling it, but otherwise it was boring mom-talk so Will figured he was safe. Then Mom asked how the Herreras were settling in since the move.

Mrs. Herrera said Eloy's little sisters, Elsi and Melanie, were fine, but she'd been worried about Eloy until he joined the wrestling team. "We didn't realize Triton doesn't have a soccer team."

"You play soccer?" Will asked Eloy.

Eloy shrugged.

His mom sighed a little. "I think his dad loves soccer more than Eloy does."

"You can play for *hours* and no one wins," Eloy said. "Wrestling?" He smacked a hand onto the counter. "You make a pin. Done."

Will agreed. Wrestling had a clarity a lot of other things in life didn't. "He's pretty good, too," he told Mrs. Herrera.

But admitting it in front of Eloy was too hard to let stand. "For someone who doesn't know anything."

Eloy thumped Will's arm.

Will thumped back.

"I can take him home now," Mom pretended to offer Mrs. Herrera. "My son may not be mature enough for a play date."

"Ha-ha," Will said.

Mrs. Herrera smiled. "Well, if he decides to stick with the wrestling, we've worked it out."

"I'm sticking with it, *Mamá*," Eloy said, as if he was upset she'd said anything.

Will thought she meant rides and stuff, but Eloy's tone made it seem as if there was more to it. "What?" he asked, looking back and forth between Eloy and his mom.

Mrs. Herrera glanced at Eloy as if she was sorry she'd mentioned it, but she explained, "We usually visit my husband's family in Oaxaca over the holidays."

Will didn't get it. It wasn't like they wrestled on Christmas or New Year's or anything.

"It's a long trip, so we arrange things with the school to stay for a month," she added.

"But that's right in the middle of wrestling!" Will didn't mean to shout, but December and January were the deepest part of the season, with meets every Thursday night and all-day tournaments every Saturday. If Eloy was gone a whole month, even not counting winter break, he'd miss a ton of matches.

"We've got it worked out," Eloy said, his jaw tightened into that square it got when he was ticked.

"By missing half the season?"

"Will," Will's mom said.

"My dad's coming back early with me," Eloy said.

"Oh, great! Why didn't you just say?" Then Will realized what that meant. "Oh."

All four of his own grandparents lived nearby, Mom's parents there in town and Dad's over in Faribault. Will saw them for everything—all the holidays and birthdays and anniversaries and a lot of Hollie's games and Will's meets and other times just because. Aunts, uncles, cousins—everybody was pretty much around all the time. Even the ones in La Crosse were only an hour and a half away. He couldn't imagine what it would be like if half of them were so far away, he only saw them once or twice a year, especially one of his grandmas. And both Eloy and Mr. Herrera were going to cut that time short.

"I'm sorry." That wasn't the right thing to say exactly, but he didn't know what was.

"It's cool." Eloy shrugged, but Will wasn't fooled. Eloy might have chosen to come back early, but he'd definitely given up some time that was important to him. Eloy grabbed a couple of bottles of Gatorade from the fridge. "You ready?"

"Uh, yeah."

Mom said her good-byes and reminded Will when she'd be back to get him. Will smiled at Mrs. Herrera and Elsi, then followed Eloy to a finished basement. On the way, he remembered Eloy's dig from earlier. "I do know the Spanish alphabet. I'm not a complete, uh, *menso*," he said, repeating what had to have been an insult. To prove it, he recited, "*Ah, bay, say, day, eh, ehfay—*"

"Please stop hurting my ears."

Will dropped his gym bag and grabbed Eloy in a loose headlock, pretending to wrestle him to the ground.

Eloy executed a decent escape, wrapping his arms around Will and lifting him off his feet. Fortunately, Eloy didn't follow through with the turn. The drop to the ground would have landed Will flat on his back. "You forgot *chay, menso*," Eloy said.

Which meant that practice was on.

They wrestled for nearly two hours, moves the coaches had shown them, others Will knew, and a couple Eloy had found on YouTube. After Will told Eloy what had happened with the crickets, they didn't say much, though Will had stuff he might have wanted to talk about if Eloy seemed up for it. The big one, of course, was whether Eloy thought he really would stick with wrestling. It wasn't that Will didn't feel comfortable with most of the other guys, but it was kind of nice to not be the youngest one on the team.

Wrestling was hard. The season was a grind of six days a week practice, meets, tournaments. Making weight, maintaining gear, travel. Muscles tired. Brain tired. Desire to win tired. Eloy didn't know how tough it got. Will did.

So what if, as practices got harder and included more and more serious wrestling, Eloy changed his mind? It wasn't as if he had nothing else to do. He could go to Mexico for a month and hang out with his family and miss school, too, which sounded cool. It sounded way better than wrestling through a long Minnesota winter.

Thinking about Eloy coming back early with his dad reminded Will he was supposed to meet Mr. Herrera, too.

"So, um, is your dad here?" The idea of meeting the best cook ever in real life filled Will's stomach with moths.

Eloy laughed and pointed at Will. "Your face. He's just my dad."

"'Just'?" Eloy's dad was chef of El Corazón. "You didn't really think I came here to wrestle, did you? You said I'd get to meet him."

"You will. I heard him come in with Melanie a while ago."

"And you kept me here in the basement?!"

"We *were* practicing," Eloy said to Will's back. As he climbed the stairs, Will smoothed his sweaty hair and straightened his T-shirt and shorts, groaned when he realized he still had on his dorky-looking kneepads, then reached the top and smacked straight into Mr. Herrera.

Eloy's dad quickly shifted one of the drinks he was holding to the other hand and grabbed Will's arm to keep him from tumbling backward down the stairs, but Will had already over-corrected forward to keep his balance—too far forward—and he basically fell into a hug with Mr. Herrera.

Laughing, Mr. Herrera thumped Will's back before stepping back. "Will Nolan! It's great to meet you."

Mr. Herrera kept his black hair close cut, like a wrestler, but he had a beard, too, graying on his chin. Technically, Will had "met" Mr. Herrera at the restaurant when the man stopped by people's tables to say hi and ensure that they were enjoying their meals—as if they might not. But there, he was the awesome chef, not Eloy's dad, a person Will might know in real life.

"You, too." Will suddenly felt shy, but his stomach didn't; it rumbled loudly, making Mr. Herrera laugh again.

"You worked up an appetite. Good! I brought you some *tejate*."

The fact Eloy lunged for the drink even though he got to eat his dad's cooking all the time was an extra-good sign that was proved true when Will took his first sip.

Tejate was kind of like a thin milk shake, but not milky, with faint chocolate and cinnamon flavors and something else he didn't know. He couldn't describe it except it was basically a drink of the gods. He knew he should pause to breathe and thank Mr. Herrera but he was too busy guzzling every drop, just like Eloy.

"It's not quite *tejate*," Mr. Herrera said. "*That* you find only on the streets in Oaxaca, but my recipe is not so bad, eh?"

Will and Eloy nodded, wiping foam mustaches from their lips.

"If that is only 'not so bad,'" Will said, "I *have* to go to Oaxaca someday. Like, tomorrow."

Eloy rolled his eyes, but Mr. Herrera laughed. "Practice was good?"

"Yes, sir. Eloy's getting pretty good," Will said, and this time he didn't follow up the comment with a razz the way he had when he'd said the same thing to Eloy's mom.

"I didn't expect him to choose wrestling," Mr. Herrera admitted, "but I'm glad to see him make friends." He squeezed Eloy's shoulder. "I know the move was hard."

"Um, yes, sir," Will said again. After wrestling together the last few days, Will had kind of forgotten that Eloy was a new kid. It was weird thinking about him having an old school and maybe a bunch of friends and now being at a new school where the only person Will had really seen Eloy hanging out with was . . . Will. It wasn't that Eloy didn't talk to anyone else, but it had to be hard fitting into a place where pretty much everyone had known one another since they were little kids Elsi's age.

Will slanted a glance at Eloy, who rolled his eyes again.

Mr. Herrera turned back to Will, eyes twinkling. "So, you're a wrestler and a gastronome, eh?"

"Uh . . ." Will wanted to get along with Mr. Herrera—he wanted to get along *great* with Mr. Herrera—but since he wasn't sure what a gastronome was, he didn't know how to answer the question.

"He means 'foodie,'" Eloy said.

"Oh! Yes! *Your* food, Mr. Herrera. Anything you make. Ever."

Eloy snorted. "Fangirl."

Mr. Herrera only laughed again and put an arm over Will's shoulders. "I like you. And the *chapulines*, you will like them."

"I know I will," Will agreed, not letting himself wince at the image that popped into his head of a giant grasshopper eating *him*. "Thank you so much for helping."

"Like I said, I'm glad to see my son make friends at his new school." He squeezed Will a little harder, and Will wondered if he was imagining the feeling that Mr. Herrera's comment had something more behind it. Did he know that Will and Eloy had bargained grasshoppers for help with wrestling? That wasn't exactly the kind of thing *friends* did, but Eloy was Will's teammate now, and that was just as good, wasn't it?

Mrs. Herrera called out that Will's mom had pulled into

the drive, so Will went back downstairs to get his stuff together. Eloy followed him and cleared his throat. "I was thinking. Mr. Taylor would probably let us work together on one big presentation."

Will's foot caught in the sweaty kneepad he was finally sliding off. He stumbled sideways.

In theory, it would be cool to have a partner on the project, because they could split the work. But the suggestion gave him a queasy feeling. He had an idea that him eating a bug in front of the class was different from Eloy doing so. It wasn't fair, and maybe not true, but he'd been caught off guard by what Darryl had said, and he didn't want to find out if there were other people who would surprise him, too.

"Yeah, but Mr. Taylor would probably make us do twice as many slides," Will said. Class presentations had to have at least ten slides, which meant each student came up with precisely ten slides, and even geeks didn't go over.

"And you *are* a bug eater," Eloy said, tugging off his damp T-shirt and pulling on a hoodie. "I probably shouldn't associate with you any more than I have to."

Will uncurled the sweaty elastic band of the kneepad in his hand. Eloy was turned away, closing the laptop they'd watched the wrestling demonstrations on and bundling his own kneepads with his T-shirt. Will felt as if he was supposed to say something. Actually, he knew he was supposed to say something, but he didn't want to say it. He didn't want them to do the presentation together. If they did, it wasn't only that Will would take a ton of crap from Darryl. Eloy might, too.

So instead he said, "You really are picking it up fast."

Eloy looked at the stuff in his hands. "Huh?"

"Wrestling," Will said. "You're doing great."

"It's hard not to be inspired." He held up his copy of *Wrestling for Dummies*, page corners already folded down.

Will peered at it but didn't get what Eloy meant.

Eloy pointed at the author's name. "Henry Cejudo. One of the youngest American wrestlers to win an Olympic gold medal. His mom emigrated from Mexico."

Will stared at the book cover. All he'd ever noticed about the wrestler pictured on the front was his stance and how intense he looked. He hadn't actually thought about *who* the guy was.

Eloy shook his head. "You didn't even read the bio, did you?"

"The book does say it's for dummies," Will joked.

Eloy shook his head but had to bite back a smile.

CRICKETS CHIRPED WILL ON AS HE SPENT THE REST OF the weekend researching grasshoppers, downloading pictures, and starting to put together slides for his science presentation even though he still had another whole week to prepare and usually wouldn't have started so early. There was so much good stuff, it was tough to choose what would go into his ten slides—he easily could have done twenty. But he'd never exceed the minimum and be accused of worse than geekdom.

Back at school Monday morning, Will unloaded books from his backpack.

And freed half a dozen crickets.

He banged his forehead on a locker door, repeatedly.

"Bug Boy strikes again!" Simon said. He nudged a cricket that hadn't taken off yet and hooted when it arced through the air. He poked into Will's backpack. "What are you doing with the others?"

Will froze, head still pressed against the metal lockers, cold seeping into his brain. He turned slowly. "So it *was* you?"

"A *thousand* crickets? Of course it was me! So what will you do with them?"

Will imagined "nudging" Simon and watching *him* arc through the air. "Why didn't you warn me?"

"Are you kidding? I wish I could have seen your face. A thousand crickets are funny!"

"Not when they escaped in my house and I had to *kill* them!"

Simon blinked so fast, his eyelids could have flown away. But then he started to grin. "They . . . escaped?"

"It's not funny." Will ripped out his social studies book and jammed his backpack into the locker.

"I was going to text you about them, but you didn't have your phone," Simon said. "Are you mad at me, like, for real?"

"Hundreds of cricket corpses, Simon." Will said. "Hundreds. And they stink." The smell was like roadkill from a distance. Though the traps didn't catch many crickets anymore, there were still plenty in the house— their chirps echoed through the night.

"What did you do now, losers?" Darryl leaned against a locker, acting extra casual.

Will darted an instinctive glance toward Eloy's locker,

but he wasn't around, which was strange but for the moment kind of OK.

Ever since Darryl had stomped off to the library last week, he and Will had been weird together but trying to act normal until they got back to normal. Calling one another losers was an ordinary thing, a razz just because.

But after killing all those crickets, Will felt like a loser for real. He tried to shrug it off. "Simon sent me a box of crickets."

"What was he supposed to do with them?" Darryl asked Simon.

"Exactly," Will said.

Then a boy shrieked and a girl laughed as a cricket bounded down the hall. "Bug Boy!" they shouted in unison but in two completely different tones.

"*That's* what he was supposed to do with them," Simon said, waving his arms like giant tentacles. "We released the kraken!"

"It looked like three crickets," Darryl said.

"Crickets of doom!"

Will shook his head and grabbed his stuff for social studies. The library was supposed to be open again today, and they were supposed to go there. He glanced nervously in that direction. "How was it in there?" he asked Darryl.

Darryl followed Will's gaze and grinned. "Not a war zone. The school's stupid for making such a big deal out of it."

Not stupid so much as following rules about kids and

pesticides and stuff, but Will agreed because he wanted a little bit of feeling normal again. "Yeah."

Then another shriek sounded, this one only a few feet behind him and piercing enough to make him jump.

"Girls," Darryl snorted. He didn't have a sister who would bop him for talking that way.

Will almost didn't turn around. Though the halls were often filled with shrieks and shouts, this one had that extra something to it that made him ninety-nine percent sure it was inspired by one of the crickets he'd "unleashed." He still felt bad about them. Yesterday, when he'd handed over the bag of crickets he'd taken to Diggy's, they'd looked roughed up—gray, broken, and small—and Diggy's expression had been doubtful that his steer would be willing to eat them. At least when Will and his classmates ate the grasshoppers, their deaths would be for a reason. Will wasn't a baby about bugs, but it seemed so pointless for a *thousand* crickets to bite it for no reason.

But Simon was a funny guy, and the crickets probably would have been funny, too, somehow, if they hadn't escaped. And actually, Will had to admit he'd be laughing his head off if it had happened to someone else.

So Will turned, his Bug-Boy arms raised to claim the cricket and bestow a buggy blessing on the latest classmate to be touched by an angel/arthropod, only to hear instead, "Hollie! You . . . you . . . have a huge bug in your hair!"

Hollie stood by her locker, wide-eyed, ponytail swinging

frantically as she looked all around herself. Sometimes Will forgot they went to school in the same building. But he got a bad feeling and took a step toward her as she said, "Where? Where is it?"

"It's in back now!"

Hollie grabbed her ponytail, pulling the end in front of her face—and the live cricket right beneath her nose.

She shrieked and instinctively threw the ponytail away from her, but all that did was swing it around her back and slap it onto the other side of her neck. The contact made her shudder away in a spastic dance, but she couldn't get away from her own hair.

"How could you not know you had a *bug* in your hair?" her friend Amy screeched, not being helpful at all, while Kathryn held out her hands, trying to calm Hollie.

It hit Will just how much Hollie had been creeped out by the crickets this weekend—and that she'd helped him anyway.

"I'll get it," Will said. He got a hold of her ponytail, but her shaking had tangled it into a jungle for the creature to hide in. "It'll be easier if I spread it out," he told her, pulling down the elastic band.

"No!" she yelled just before he heard the pop and crunch as he accidentally squished the cricket's guts into her hair.

Air left the hall as everyone sucked it in. Even people too

far away to know what was going on quieted, sensing the charge in the atmosphere like a tornado warning.

Hollie heaved, once, as if she wanted to throw up but held it down, slowly turning to look at Will.

He waited for her to say she was going to kill him, that he was an idiot, that payback was a great and terrible thing.

Instead, her face wrinkled in that way he recognized from living with two women his entire life: She was going to cry.

She held that back, too, for now and pushed her way through the circle around her, walking fast but not letting herself run toward the bathroom.

Everyone let her go.

"I don't get how she didn't *know*," Amy repeated. "She had a *giant bug* in her *hair*."

"Shut up!" Will shouted.

Before Amy could yell back at him, Kathryn glared at Will. "Did you put it there, *Bug Boy*?"

"What? No!" Hollie was his sister, which meant, of course, that she got on his nerves and on his case about stupid stuff all the time, but jeez. What kind of person did they think he was?

"It would have been funny if he had," Darryl said, making Will stare. Did Darryl think he was defending Will, or could he actually mean it?

"It's my fault," Simon said. "It probably hitchhiked in her bag like the ones that came with Will today."

"What are you even talking about?" Kathryn snapped at Simon.

"The thousand crickets I sent Will," Simon said, as if he was surprised that everyone didn't already know. "The ones that escaped in their house?"

"Hollie has a thousand crickets all over her house?" Amy shrieked.

"Gross," another eighth grader said.

"They probably crawled all over her while she slept," some guy said, making Amy and a couple of other girls shrink away as if giant crickets were coming to get them.

"You eat eight spiders a year in your sleep," another guy said.

"That's an urban legend," Will said.

"I bet she ate that many crickets in one night," the guy said.

"Shut. Up." Kathryn pushed her way through the circle, pulling a reluctant Amy with her and knocking into Will harder than she needed to. "Thanks a lot, Bug Boys," she said, adding Simon and Darryl to her glare.

"I'm no Bug Boy," Darryl said to her back as she headed to the bathroom Hollie was in.

Will wanted to protest, too, though not about being a Bug Boy. Hollie hadn't done anything but have him for a brother, and now she was paying for it. He hoped those guys were only teasing and weren't suddenly going to treat his sister as if she had cooties or something. Hollie was pretty popular, he reasoned. Even if they'd sounded a little mean to him, her friends were probably only being funny. Things would go back to normal once she washed her hair.

He winced at the memory of the pop and crunch, the bug *he'd* squished in her hair. Even he was creeped out at the idea of cricket guts smeared on his head, and he'd eaten a stinkbug.

Uff da. He owed her big-time.

Will thought about waiting for her outside the bathroom to apologize, but the teachers were waving students into class, and he figured he was the last person she'd want to see anyway.

"Way to stick with the team, Darryl," Simon grumbled.

"We wouldn't have to deal with that Bug Boy crap in the first place if it wasn't for that Mexican."

"Will you *shut up* about that?" Will shouted. Jeez, he was glad Eloy still wasn't around, though he couldn't help but wonder where the guy was.

Darryl poked a finger at Will's chest, hard. "*You're* the one who ate the bug."

"That's not what I'm talking about, and you know it."

Darryl glared so hard, his eyes could have steamed. "You should remember who your friends are."

That was part of Will's problem. He *did* remember who his friends were, but he was starting to wonder if they were only memories. In Will's mind, none of his friends was the kind of person who gave a crap about where someone came from. But apparently Darryl did. So what did that mean for Will?

When Eloy stepped out of the health classroom talking with Coach Van Beek, Will snagged on his own thinking, because the thing was, Eloy might not be from Dodge Center, but Rochester was only forty minutes away, and both were in Minnesota, which was at the very top—smack in the middle—of the United States. Eloy was from "here" as much as Will, Simon, and even Darryl were.

"Hey, hey, hey." Simon half sang, half danced between Will and Darryl. "It was an accident, and Hollie's tough. I've seen her play volleyball. Everything will be back to normal tomorrow." But he gave Will a sideways look that Will had no trouble interpreting.

He knew what Simon was doing, distracting Will and Darryl from the real argument by pretending their frustration was about what had just happened to Hollie. It was the kind of misdirection that had worked before, and Will almost wanted to follow Simon's lead, because the idea of returning to normal sounded really good right about now.

But Simon's look was a reminder that, faked or real, normal was *not* going to last. Will was going to feed the class grasshoppers. Eloy was going to help him. Bug Boys would be cemented as the new normal. And as Darryl had just declared, he was no Bug Boy.

Will was starting to think he was okay with that.

ALL WEEK, THOSE FEW CRICKETS ROAMED FREE AT
school, chirping in the hall as if they could tell the acoustics
there were perfect for them. Every time the whirring
vibrato sounded, someone offered to catch the bug for Will
for a snack or asked if he wanted ant-chovy pizza or moth-
olate cake, showing that some students had taken Simon's
words to heart about getting more creative with their bug-
food names. But Will was still offered a lot of French flies,
bee-ritos, and maggot-aroni and fleas—people clearly had
their favorites.

At home, the chirping was less fun. The crickets sang
their guts out at night. Technically, the sound they made
was from rubbing their top wing across their ridged bottom
wing, kind of like a violin, and supposedly he could tell the
temperature by counting how many times they chirped in
fourteen seconds and adding forty.

Will had learned a lot about crickets in the dark hours of

not sleeping and trying to find out how to make their chorus stop.

Not enough time had passed for the story to be funny, but telling Dad about it again in person, they could see how it would be one day. Still, Dad was ticked enough for Mom and Hollie's sake that he had a long call with Simon. Simon had an uncle and older guy cousins, but he'd always especially liked Dad, so Will wasn't surprised when Simon was a little more subdued the next day.

Dad tried to stop the chirping by turning down the thermostat to fifty-five, because he read that crickets didn't chirp when they were too cold. But it was *November*, and the humans were too cold, too. The traps still worked, and each morning Will or Dad dumped a few more cricket corpses, but some hardy suckers had apparently moved into the walls. Hollie bleach-wiped her room every single day.

She didn't need to, Will knew. Though they sounded like a horde at night while people were trying to sleep, there weren't *that* many crickets remaining, and they didn't leave any visible messes. Will thought maybe Hollie was a little paranoid since the squishing incident, but it seemed that things were normal for her at school. He saw her and her friends around their lockers, and none of them was acting any weirder than girls usually did. Besides, Hollie was Hollie—she never really needed his help with anything anyway.

Simon's mom did ground him, but it never stuck when she did that. She worked weird hours, so it was tough to enforce anything. She was a nurse at the Mayo Clinic in Rochester, actually, and it struck Will, thinking about how Eloy's family had moved when his mom got a job with one of the Mayo Clinic's centers in Owatonna, how lucky he was that Simon's mom hadn't moved them to the city after the divorce.

"The real test will be when my dad gets the credit card bill," Simon said. Though he grinned and waggled his eyebrows, Will knew how much it bothered Simon that his dad hardly ever called, even after Simon left messages or texted him.

Will had looked up how much the crickets cost and doubted Simon's dad would be worried about a twenty-five-dollar charge. Though it was weird to hope your friend got into trouble with his dad, he said, "Who wouldn't be mad? What normal person needs a thousand crickets?"

"You, but then, you're not normal."

Will bopped Simon's arm, and Simon pretended to be mortally wounded; in other words, he was his normal self.

But on their way to class, Will heard him mutter, "He'll probably just text Mom." Will threw an arm over his friend's shoulders, and Simon let him for almost five whole seconds—a sure sign he was in a low mood—before chucking it off and claiming cooties, germs, B.O., et cetera.

In addition to lack of sleep and a little worry for Hollie and Simon, Will was dealing with the fact that wrestling practice was picking up. Now that the coaches had reminded the guys' bodies where their muscles were, sparring was added to their workouts. At first, Eloy was too hesitant, and Will felt like a meanie tackling a toddler. But Coach Van Beek got on their cases and made them step up their game.

Eloy didn't get all the rules yet, and he pulled some illegal moves, but he listened hard when Will or the coaches explained. He wasn't skilled, but he was fast and pretty strong. A few times he almost pinned Will, which would have sucked big-time. Will had wrestled for *years*; no way was the new guy taking him down, even if Will was supposed to be helping him learn how to. Next week, they'd have their first matches, and that would be the real test of how far both had come.

The science presentations were coming up next week, too.

Monday, after what had happened with Hollie and then the little dustup with Darryl, Will had thought about calling off his plan, but then Eloy mentioned that the grasshoppers were on their way from Mexico. Will hadn't thought about where Mr. Herrera would get the bugs, but he definitely wouldn't have guessed they'd be special ordered from Mexico. Eloy said it was because his dad wanted grasshoppers from Oaxaca, that he was picky about his food, and that seemed funny, since they were talking about bugs. Then Eloy said his dad wanted to be sure that Will had cleared his project with the school's food policies.

Everyone knew the drill. On TV shows, kids made homemade cupcakes or cookies for class, but that didn't happen in real life. In real life, Triton students could only bring in food "prepared commercially," per the Minnesota Department of Health. It was in the student handbook and everything. Mom said it was partly because the school got federal money, so they had to follow guidelines, but anyone who had tasted his grandma's poppy-seed bars or Mrs. Johnston's blondies cried about the injustice.

If Will's mom weren't already upset about the stinkbug and on edge about the crickets, Will might have asked her to check whether the school might make an exception in the interest of science. He definitely should have asked Mr. Taylor by now, except he knew that, as soon as he did, Mom would hear about it. And now Will didn't dare ask *anyone*, because Eloy's dad had already ordered the grasshoppers, all the way from Oaxaca! What if Will asked and was told no? He couldn't do that to Mr. Herrera. He'd simply have to take his chances.

So Will told Eloy it was all taken care of.

Which meant Will was officially stuck with his original plan whether or not he had second thoughts.

He didn't exactly mind. It was going to be funny. Through

interlibrary loan, he'd gotten a book about bug eating called *Edible* by a woman who wrote a blog called Girl Meets Bug. In it he'd found plenty of stuff to gross out his classmates but also tons of cool stuff. Everyone would eat it up—and, he hoped, eat the bugs, too.

But Will couldn't help being nervous. There'd definitely been some mixed results with bug-eating and his personal life. But he was committed now, and time did its thing and passed before he was sure he was ready.

20

THE MORNING OF THE PRESENTATION, ELOY WASN'T AT
his locker.

Not at the five-minute warning bell.

Not at the get-your-butt-to-class bell.

Eloy was supposed to bring the grasshoppers. And he wasn't there.

With Mr. Herrera involved, it seemed unlikely that Eloy had bailed, but where the heck was he? When Will had eaten that stinkbug, he'd puked. Since Mr. Herrera had made them, the grasshoppers were bound to taste decent and not make Will sick, but since he would be the first to eat one in class, he had wanted to try one on his own, just in case. Now he wondered if there would be any to eat at all.

He sat in his seat, unmoving, and stared at the door to the social studies classroom.

"Where is he?" Simon asked.

"Where's who?" Darryl grunted.

Eloy finally showed up when Mr. Hanson was halfway through taking attendance. Will wanted to leap across the room as if *he* were a grasshopper, too.

The minute class ended, Will went straight for Eloy.

"Sorry," Eloy said immediately. "I started to take the bus, but then, the garlic is pretty strong, and I thought, on the bus . . ." He flapped a hand to fill in the blank, which Will interpreted as, *I thought it wasn't a good idea to take grasshoppers on a crowded bus with a bunch of* idiotas. "But my sisters wouldn't go without me, so by the time we got home and Mom yelled at me and we loaded everyone into the car . . ." He was breathless just trying to describe it.

"Where are they now?" Will asked. Eloy had made the right decision, but Will's nerves weren't up for reassuring him right then.

"Locker."

"You got them?" Simon asked.

"Got what?" Darryl asked.

Will really wanted to put Simon in a headlock for letting Darryl follow him when he *knew* why Will needed to talk to Eloy alone.

"What do you need from *him*?" Darryl demanded.

Simon winced, finally figuring out what he'd done, though not sure what to do about it now.

Eloy just looked at Darryl.

"Wrestling stuff," Will said.

Simon jumped in, grabbing Darryl's arm to lead him away. "Jockstraps! Spandex! We've got to get out of here before we see something we can't ever forget!"

Darryl squinted at Will.

"My eyes!" Simon wailed. "They burn!"

"You haven't seen anything yet, loser," Darryl said. He shook his head at Will before leading the fake-crying Simon away.

"Wrestling stuff, huh?" Eloy said to Will. He didn't sound mad. He didn't have to. After two weeks together wrestling, on the mats six days a week, Will had gotten to know Eloy's tone of voice.

"He'll come around," Will said.

Eloy shrugged. "I don't care." He seemed to mean it, too, reminding Will of that time Eloy had said he didn't want to be friends with Darryl. Will got why, but it still felt weird.

There were people who annoyed him, but even guys he didn't hang out with were still kind of his friends. That's what happened when you grew up with the same hundred or so people. You were in the same classes year after year, and you knew all their crap the way they knew yours.

"What do you think is going to happen after the presentation?" Eloy asked.

"Huh?"

"With your friend?"

He meant Darryl, and Will felt a moment of panic, because he really didn't know, but then Eloy opened his locker, and out wafted scents of garlic, chili, and lime. Will pulled in a deep breath and forgot everything else, because he did know one thing for sure.

He was about to give the best class presentation *ever*.

BECAUSE WILL HAD FRESH "FOOD," HE'D ASKED TO GO first, which had raised Mr. Taylor's eyebrows practically off his head. The reaction was kind of disappointing, because Will tried hard in science, but he supposed it was fair. Will had suffered through class presentations for years himself, and most people had to be forced to take their turns. Really, he was lucky Mr. Taylor wasn't overly suspicious.

While Mr. Taylor took attendance, Will felt as if someone were pulling his belly button through his back. Once he got started, he was sure he'd be fine. Pretty sure. Like, mostly. He just needed to get started. But after attendance, Mr. Taylor reviewed the assignment itself, reminding everyone that they'd be learning about insects' roles in the environment and biodiversity, including each particular insect's impact on humans, and Will realized he had completely forgotten the details of the *actual assignment*. As soon as

Mr. Taylor had mentioned "insects" and "presentation" that first time, Will had stopped focusing, blown away by the possibility of awesomeness and how to make his plan work. Will's presentation definitely included an impact on humans, but pretty much *nothing else*. Will couldn't fail *science*, a class taught by one of his *wrestling coaches*. What the heck had he been thinking?! Maybe he could back out of going first, tell Mr. Taylor he needed more time. If he went last, he could—

A small paper wad thwacked his cheek.

Eloy mouthed, "Breathe."

Simon patted Will's shoulder.

Darryl crushed a full sheet of paper into a tight, hard ball and glared at Eloy.

"Don't," Will whispered.

Darryl tapped the ball on his desk while Will practiced that whole breathing thing again and Mr. Taylor listed the few people who still had to send in their files. When they had class presentations, everyone uploaded their slides to a shared drive so the teachers could point and click to project them onto the whiteboard. Will had waited to upload his late the night before so Mr. Taylor wouldn't have time to look at it beforehand. Will doubted that teachers had the time or energy to preview student presentations *and* listen to them in class—talk about *bor-ing*—but Will hadn't wanted to risk it.

Remembering how dull class presentations always were calmed Will down some.

If his presentation was going to be anything, it wouldn't be boring.

When Mr. Taylor finally invited Will to the front, the class quieted, sitting straighter in their seats or even leaning forward. He knew they expected something extra from him because the entire assignment had been inspired by him, but now it hit him: They *anticipated* it. Nerves wormed around his throat.

As Will slowly stood up, Eloy gave him a man nod.

Darryl crossed his arms.

Simon stood and bowed, gesturing Will to the front of the room as if he were a great magician or something.

A few people giggled, enough to propel Will forward and signal Mr. Taylor for the first slide—a photo of four cows dressed like a cowboy, a cop, a construction worker, and an Indian, like the band that sang "YMCA."

The class hooted and laughed until Mr. Taylor gave them *the look*.

Will grinned.

Bug Boy's time had come.

"Cows poop," he began. People grinned and groaned in about equal numbers. "But worse, they burp."

"A burp is worse than poop?" Cristian asked as if he'd been coached.

"Thank you for asking, my friend," Will said. "Cow burps are methane, and those burps add thirty percent more greenhouse gases to the environment than cars do."

"You telling us to give up cows?" Darryl asked.

"Don't take my steak from me!" Simon hollered.

"Or ice cream," Megan added.

Will put a hand over his heart. "I would never suggest anything like that. I'm merely pointing out that cows, while tasty, do create some environmental problems. Like, they require ten pounds of food to make one pound of meat."

Eyes widened as a few guessed what he was getting at. He gestured for the next slide, the cover of a book, and read the title aloud, "Edible: An Adventure into the World of Eating Insects and the Last Great Hope to Save the World."

The class lost it, laughing or forcefully declaring they would *never*, a good sign that they *would* when he suggested it.

"Cows are great, but there are seven and a half billion people on the planet now, and already a lot of them starve." Will paused because that part wasn't funny; it was scary. "In 2050, we'll have almost *ten* billion people. Some of you will be as old as our parents, and your kids will be in this same class."

Mr. Taylor put his head in his hands and muttered, "Lord, help me."

"Cows, pigs, chickens—they just won't be enough food

for everyone. But you can grow enough insects in your backyard, your closet, or even under your bed to feed you and your family for the rest of your life."

A chorus of "Not me!" almost drowned out Darryl's muttered, "Someone should feed *you* to the bugs under *your* bed."

Will tried not to picture Darryl actually doing that. He cleared his throat. "The thing is, all of you already *do* eat bugs, all the time."

Nuh-uh's filled the air as the whiteboard lit with the next slide—photos of a bottle of ketchup, a jar of peanut butter, a Hershey bar, and a slice of pizza.

He pointed to the neck of the ketchup bottle. This part was so gross and so cool. "You know how a lot of bottles have this paper ring around the cap, like ketchup and salad dressing and stuff? They started putting that on in the old days, to hide the black layer of bug parts that floated to the top."

A few people pretended to gag. "The Food and Drug Administration has a giant list of how many bug parts— or worse things, like wood chips, animal hair, and even poop—can be in food and still be safe." Will explained that a quarter cup of peanut butter or half cup of chocolate could legally contain thirty insect fragments. A slice of pizza could safely have one hundred fifty in the crust, plus thirty fly eggs in the tomato sauce. If one's dad had a beer with it, he would drink *twenty-five hundred* aphids, too. And that was only the insect parts. He couldn't help but shudder a little himself. "Everyone eats one or two pounds of insects a year, especially if you eat a lot of prepackaged stuff. In your lifetime, you'll basically eat an insect as big as Mr. Taylor."

"Well, I'm never eating again," Mackala said.

"Never say never!" Will grinned, pointing at one of the images on the next slide of a guy with a scorpion on a stick. "If you've ever been to the state fair, you know how good food-on-a-stick is." Gesturing at the other pics of people eating tarantulas, grasshoppers, and worms, he added, "People all over the world eat all kinds of bugs."

"Because they're too stupid to know any better," Darryl said.

"Because they don't have anything else to eat," Simon countered before Mr. Taylor got a chance to snap at Darryl.

Eloy, Cristian, and Megan glared at them both.

Without knowing it, they were talking about the food Mr. Herrera had prepared. Will expected that crap from Darryl but not Simon. And now Eloy was looking at Will, foot tapping, like he'd *better* say something, or else. Will cleared his throat. "Actually, in many places, bugs are delicacies and cost *mucho dinero*."

Eloy did a facepalm, with feeling.

Will wanted to throw up his hands and say, *What?* He'd corrected Darryl and Simon, hadn't he? But Joshua spoke first. "Delicacies in other places. Not here."

"Yes, here, too," Will said, glad to move on. He pointed to the photos on the next slide. "There's the Tiny Termite Café at the Insectarium in New Orleans, the Black Ant restaurant in New York City, Don Bugito food trucks in California, and lots of companies here in the United States that sell mealworm flour and make energy bars and chips from crickets and stuff like that. Entomophagy"—he pronounced it carefully: *en-tuh-MOFF-ah-gee*—"is eating insects for food on purpose, and it's a real thing."

The next slide said only, "$1,082,200." Quite a few leaned forward at that kind of payday.

Will left them dangling for a moment. "Bugs are serious business. In 2013, the United Nations recommended that we eat more of them. They have loads of nutrients that are good for us, and because they don't need a lot of resources like land, water, and food to grow, they're good for the planet, too."

"What's that got to do with a million bucks?" Simon asked.

"That's how much money one guy got paid just to study bugs as food. So, how *do* you eat them?" Will asked.

"You don't," Darryl barked.

"You're the expert," Tyler piped up.

"Yeah, he is!" Simon crowed.

The next slide had a long list of insects and a rhyme from *The Eat-a-Bug Cookbook* by David George Gordon. "'Red, orange, or yellow, forgo this small fellow. Black, green, or brown, go ahead and toss him down.' Basically, you shouldn't pick up any ol' bug off the street or eat them raw, but there are more than 1,900 edible ones. I couldn't list them all here, but there are ants and beetles, including *dung* beetles, caterpillars, *cockroaches*, worms, flies, termites, and, of course, *stinkbugs*."

After his experience, Will had been surprised to see stinkbugs on the list, but apparently if you didn't tick them off first and make them spray in your mouth, they had an apple flavor. Go figure.

The class cheered him on, and the next slide made them laugh more. *Starship Troopers* was an old movie about giant alien insects waging war on the universe. Will had found great pics: a tank-size beetle coming out of the ground, grasshoppers twice as big as humans attacking a compound, and a cool mantis-like bug sucking out a human brain.

"If this doesn't inspire you to eat bugs, nothing will. There are *two hundred million* insects per *single human* on the planet. That's three hundred pounds of insects per one pound of human. For me, that's *thirty thousand pounds* of insects. They outnumber us by so much that in a bug apocalypse, they'd win."

He let that sink in before nodding for the second-to-last slide, a recipe for *chapulines* and a photo of a market in Oaxaca de Juárez, where grasshoppers were piled high on big round trays the size of tables.

"If we're going to win the bugocalypse," Will said dramatically, "we must act now."

"Act how?" Simon asked.

"By eating as many insects as we can."

THE CHITTERING, LAUGHING, PROTESTING CLASS FELL silent.

Will raised a brown bag and slowly pulled out a transparent Tupperware container, holding it up for all to see. Reddish-brown lumps shifted inside, almost as if they were alive. As he let the bag fall to the floor, the air was scented with the tang of lime, a bite of garlic, and the warmth of chili. Will's stomach rumbled loudly enough for all to hear.

"He's really going to do it," Mackala said. "Again."

"Don't you ever learn, Will Nolan?" Megan said, not so much mean as exasperated, making Will pause.

He'd had second thoughts about his plan a couple of times, but once he'd started researching, he got really excited. It wasn't only that bug eating got him laughs, but that everything he'd learned was *true*. Entomophagy was good for people and the planet. The Triton students all lived in farm country: corn, soybeans, turkeys and pigs, more corn. Sure, he was talking about bugs, not plants or animals, but raising food was what they did out here, so it wasn't completely crazy to think that farmers might get into the idea, was it?

Besides, eating that stinkbug should have been worse than eating a booger, with a mandatory minimum of social humiliation. Instead, he'd become popular. Whether they meant it or not, his classmates were already halfway on board with his idea.

"Wait a minute, Will," Mr. Taylor said, asking Will if he had actually gotten permission from any school official to bring food to class.

"I swear, these insects are fine to eat, and they're educational, too," Will said quickly. "The principal definitely approves of nutritious, educational food."

Mr. Taylor didn't seem convinced, but he hesitated, looking at a class that was actually interested in a presentation for once, so Will jumped in.

He gave the container a gentle shake. "These tasty treats are called *chap-pew-leen-ays*."

"*Chap-oo-LEEN-ess*," Eloy muttered.

"What he said," Will agreed. "And we are going to eat them."

The silence was complete. No chairs squeaked. No clothes rustled. No lungs breathed.

Then a *tat-tat-tat* arose as Darryl rapped on his desk the tight paper ball he'd wadded.

Will swallowed at the air suddenly clogging his throat.

Darryl squeezed the paper ball even tighter, leaning back, legs spread out, and eyes lasered on Will.

Eloy's jaw was a hard square. The purposeful way he kept his eyes directly forward made it clear he was aware of Darryl's mood and was not looking that way again.

Will looked back and forth between the two of them.

How had he convinced himself it was "safer" for Eloy to do his own presentation than to team up with Will? The stinkbug thing had been *because* of Eloy. *Of course* Darryl would think Will had chosen a side. Will didn't want to be on any sides, but his last slide might as well be a declaration: It thanked Mr. Herrera and recommended that everyone go to his restaurant.

Now Will had the grasshoppers, and he had to eat one. There was no going back.

And he wasn't sure he wanted to go back.

Darryl and he had been friends for a long time, but would a real friend make him feel crappy for trying to be a decent person? Shouldn't the friend want to be decent, too?

Titters sounded, alerting Will he'd been quiet too long.

"Scared?" Darryl asked.

Will's smile was hard as he whipped off the container's lid. A poof of chili made him sneeze and the class laugh. It gave him the encouragement he needed.

The thing about eating the stinkbug was, he hadn't been

looking into its eyes and thinking, "I'm going to eat you." The grasshoppers, though—they seemed to be looking at *him*.

Though they were clearly dead and wonderfully cooked, they still had *legs* and *wings* and EYES, and now that he was used to the smell of garlic, lime, and chili, he caught another smell, like . . . earthworms on a rainy day? The bugs looked like mutant shrimp, and it hit him again: He had to eat one.

A glance around the classroom was not reassuring. Why was everything so gray? The walls were covered with posters, but the floor, the desks, the cinder blocks were all gray. Gray winter light stayed behind the windows, not bothering to come in, and outside, the grass was old and gray, too. It was pointless to hope his face wasn't gray. It had to be. Everything here was gray, even the grasshoppers beneath their dusting of spices.

The grasshoppers were about half the size of his thumb, with short wings pressed tight against plump, segmented bellies. Long hind legs were thick, ready to jump. Broken antennae hung over round, shiny, black compound eyes.

Desks squeaked, prodding him.

He picked up a *chapulín*, displayed it to the class . . .

. . . and popped it into his mouth.

Being in his mouth did not magically transform it into food. It still felt like a grasshopper—poking legs and antennae and shell-like exoskeleton. But as the flavors of chili, garlic, and lime curled around his tongue, he was encouraged. No matter what, this would be a hundred times better than eating the stinkbug—probably a thousand times better.

And it was. He crunched down to a spongy inside, and something squirted from one end—he could guess which one—but it was salty and citrusy and kind of . . . earthy, like grass and worms in a weirdly OK way. The texture was harder to get used to, almost like those yellow bits of popcorn kernels but with legs. In the end, he decided it was like eating unpeeled shrimp. The best part was, he knew it wasn't going to make him puke. He threw his arms up in a V.

The class roared and stamped and clapped, inspiring him to grab another grasshopper and bite it in half, letting bug juice drip down his chin. Filled with power, he walked to Darryl's desk and shook the container under his nose, making the insects look alive. "Your turn."

It wasn't until the words left his mouth that he remembered the last time he'd said them to Darryl—after Will had taken the stinkbug dare Darryl had dodged. The memory made the words feel aggressive, which he was fine with when Darryl glared at him.

"Just because you're too stupid to know better doesn't mean I am."

"Suuure," Will said, tossing the remaining half of the grasshopper into his mouth. It was the second time his tough friend had backed away from a dare. The fact that

Will hadn't, either time, made it that much worse, and both of them knew it.

"My turn," Simon shouted. He jumped up and had his hand in the container before Will finished turning around. Three grasshoppers went into his mouth.

Cristian and Joshua sensibly took one apiece, studying it from all angles before biting in.

Megan and Mackala laid theirs on neatly folded squares of brown paper towel.

Devontae pretended to be attacked by his, then ate it in "self-defense."

Adam ate with his mouth open so everyone could see the guts and legs and wings.

A bunch of people came back for more, already telling one another the epic tales of their bug-eating adventures, practicing what they would say to friends and the sad kids who had missed out *again*. They were all part of the story this time, shining in Bug Boy's reflection, and word would spread far and fast.

Will walked around the desks, offering grasshoppers and asking how they were, enjoying playing host and laughing when Simon played snobby but approving food critic. Will was back at his desk before he noticed that Eloy hadn't taken any *chapulines*. Instead, he sat there looking straight ahead, jaw clenched so tight, his teeth could break.

ELOY'S EXPRESSION ANNOYED THE HECK OUT OF WILL.
The presentation had ended exactly as they'd hoped, with
everyone eating bugs. The slide thanking Mr. Herrera was
still up on the whiteboard. And whether he'd intended it or
not, Will had picked a side today—and it hadn't been his
oldest friend's but the new guy's. The least Eloy could do
was chill.

Rustles from the hall signaled the end of class, and a
bunch of guys rushed Will to grab more *chapulines* before
darting outside to tell people what had happened. By the
time Will had his balance again, the container was empty,
and several grasshoppers littered the floor, flat and wet
from squished guts. He suspected he'd see more like that
in the hallway and felt bad. The little guys had already been
sacrificed for food; they shouldn't be wasted, too.

Mr. Taylor quickly followed the others out, shouting not

to throw food in the hall, even though he surely meant the bugs. Eloy stomped to the front of the class, picked up the Tupperware lid, and held out a hand to Will.

"What's wrong with you?" Will asked as he handed over the bottom half of the plastic container.

Eloy jerked it from his hand, put the top on the container, put the container into the brown paper bag, put the bag on his books, and headed for the door.

"Are you mad?" Will half shouted. "They loved them!"

Everyone in their entire class—minus Darryl, of course—*had eaten a bug. No one* could have predicted that a few weeks ago. In fact, a few weeks ago, Will and the entire seventh grade would have bet all their money that they would *never* eat a bug. But Will had made it happen. It had cost him, too. Eloy had gotten Will to help him with wrestling, and Will had seriously ticked off Darryl. Plus, El Corazón had gotten a lot of free advertising. Eloy should be *thanking* Will.

Already, the hall was filled with people loudly boasting about their bravery and heckling the timid. Will should be out there, too, reveling in his moment, or else what was the point of the whole thing?

"So?" he said, crossing his arms.

"Listen to them out there," Eloy said. "It's one big joke. *My dad's cooking.*"

Will flinched, arms falling at the accusation. How could

Eloy have witnessed the total success of Will's plan and drawn the conclusion that his father had been embarrassed instead? "Your dad's awesome. I would never—"

"Use our culture to make people laugh and dare each other like *chapulines* are disgusting and abnormal?"

"That is not what happened." Will couldn't even . . . After everything, he couldn't even . . . "I made it *fun.*"

"Fun*ny,* you mean."

"They wouldn't have gone near them if I—" He cut his eyes at Eloy, a thought occurring to him. "So tell me, when you went to Mexico and ate a grasshopper the first time, you didn't freak out about it?"

Eloy looked down, toeing a smushed *chapulín* and proving Will's theory correct. "I was little." Then he looked up again, eyes bright. "But my grandma gave it to me, so I tried it, and it was fine."

"This was basically the same thing. You trusted her. They trusted me. And no one would have tried them if I hadn't done it exactly the way I did."

"You don't know that. My father worked for hours."

"And I bet everyone begs to go to his restaurant now, and they'll all beg for bugs. I totally helped you," Will said. "Again."

"Don't pretend this was about me." Eloy stormed out of the room, slamming the door behind him even though Mr. Taylor was standing right outside it.

Will couldn't believe it. Intentionally or not, he had put his reputation and friendships on the line for someone he hardly knew. Now that guy was giving him grief, as if Will were somehow at fault.

The grasshoppers on the floor were dead, but he stomped on them anyway.

WILL GRADUATED FROM BUG BOY TO BUG KING.

Just like the last time, almost everyone thought he was cool and funny and awesome, and like the last time, Will tried to enjoy it. But the few people who were *not* everyone and who did *not* think he was cool and funny and awesome bugged him. He wondered if Eloy and Darryl even noticed they were on the same side now.

Practice was awkward, too. With Eloy mad and Will distracted, Eloy scored his first pin.

Will sprawled like a chalk-outline corpse. The mat reeked with new sweat, old sweat, feet, and yesterday's disinfectant.

The team cheered.

Eloy's first pin was a worthy accomplishment that deserved congratulations. Will just wished it hadn't been at his expense—or feel so much that the guys being *for* Eloy meant they were *against* Will.

Things weren't any better at home, either.

"Why the heck didn't you tell us what you were up to?" Mom asked.

"I'm sure you and Eloy had fun cooking up this idea," Dad said, "but the last time you two played with bugs, you closed down the library."

"Did it ever occur to you that parents might be upset that you fed bugs to their kids?" Mom asked.

"And some of them are blaming Mr. Herrera," Dad added, then winced, exchanging a look with Mom as if he hadn't meant to let that part slip.

"Huh? Blaming him for what?" Will asked.

"He didn't follow the school's food policy," Mom said.

Sometimes Will couldn't stand how small their living room was. He looked out the front window, but the gray day turned it into another wall. He stood looking at it anyway, with his limbs dangling at weird angles, wondering how arms ever made sense just hanging off his body the way they did.

"Mr. Herrera did ask about that," Will mumbled. "I might have told Eloy it was taken care of."

Dad's eyebrows shot up. "Might have?"

"You mean you lied," Mom said.

Will slumped onto the couch. "I don't get why anyone's mad. They all wanted to try them. I didn't force anybody." What got to Will was that the presentation had been *great*.

Not only did it go as planned, but also everyone loved it and had *tried bugs*, which was a good thing! No, he hadn't spelled out every little thing to every single person he probably should have, but he'd gotten people to try something new, something that was genuinely good for the planet.

What was he was supposed to do, apologize for helping to save the *world*?

Mom and Dad weren't sure what the school would do about the whole thing, but Mom said Principal Raymond would handle it. He was a pretty even-tempered guy. No one stayed mad around him for long.

The problem for Will was that Mr. Raymond didn't do detention or suspensions unless there was serious fighting. He said that those punishments didn't "get" him anything, preferring consequences that could provide "teachable moments." Making students spell out exactly what they had done wrong had never seemed like a big deal—until Will had to do it. Hearing his own voice detailing his bad decisions generally made them seem even stupider.

This time, though, Will didn't think he'd made any bad decisions except for lying about having gotten permission to bring food to class. He called Mr. Herrera to apologize for that, which was terrible, because, though Mr. Herrera was upset, it was more that he was disappointed. So Will felt extra crappy when he wrote the letter Mr. Raymond e-mailed to parents, explaining what he'd done so no one would blame Mr. Herrera, and he listed the real benefits of entomophagy, too, for the ones who were grossed out by the bug business.

Then he had to read an apology to Mr. Taylor and the class.

Darryl smirked the entire time and slow clapped afterward. He'd taken a seat in the back, by Devontae and Adam, and the claps vibrated over everyone's heads until Mr. Taylor made him stop.

Eloy frowned but watched Will as if he were listening hard, the way he did in wrestling when he was trying to get the particulars of a rule or move. Will stopped looking at that side of the room halfway through his reading.

Eloy wasn't right about what he'd said. Will knew how he'd meant his science presentation, and it hadn't been to make anyone a joke or seem abnormal. The high fives he got after class as he walked down the hall proved it, didn't they?

Back at their lockers, Simon only laughed about the whole thing and said it was worth it, not that he had to deal with any of "it."

Will tried to get back into the zone—people still hollered "Bug Boy!" when they saw him and offered him lice cakes and sluggy joes during lunch. But it was as if his life had taken a step to the left. Instead of Will, Darryl, and Simon sitting together, it was Will, Simon, and Joshua, who asked a thousand questions about entomophagy as if he were serious about trying it. Spotting Eloy, Joshua called him over to answer more questions. Eloy sat at the farthest corner from Will and didn't really talk to him, but they were all at the same table like they were friends. Then Megan and Mackala sat by Eloy, and even though the seats were individual stools, it felt like the girls took up more space and squished the boys together.

So he was out of it when Hollie found him later and dragged him away, startling him enough that he let her.

It was only after she hauled him around a corner that his brain caught up with events. Not only had Hollie treated him like a little kid, but she'd done it in front of his friends. And he easily could have broken her hold!

"I *so* want to smack you upside the head right now," she said.

"Like that scares me. I get thrown to the mat all the time."

"Maybe you wouldn't if you were a better wrestler."

He huffed, brain scrambling for a retort, but her talking now made him realize she hadn't said anything to him yesterday or this morning. Had she been giving him the silent treatment? Remembering the cricket guts in her ponytail last week gave him his answer and reminded him of the grasshopper guts on the floor the day before.

She was all clenched up—teeth, jaw, fists, muscles. She was a little scary. Her lip gloss and pink accessories kept tricking Will into forgetting she could kick butt. The fact that she hadn't when she clearly wanted to was probably because of the school's strict no-fighting policy, though he wondered if it applied to brothers and sisters.

"Uh, did something happen?"

"Uh, yeah," Hollie snapped. "You keep ruining my life."

"Jeezitwasonlyafewbugs." Nobody cared except the people Will cared about, which didn't make sense at all. They were supposed to be on *his* side.

Hollie slumped back against the wall. "The team doesn't want me to bake for the refreshments stand anymore."

Like most of the sports teams, the volleyball team had a booster club that sold refreshments during home games to raise money for uniforms, equipment, and whatever. School policies about prepackaged food only applied during school hours, and home-baked goods sold better than candy and chips—and Hollie's butterbeer cookies sold out no matter how many she made.

"I bet it was Amy." Will gave the wall a little kick, remembering how she'd acted when Hollie had the cricket in her hair. "Why are you even friends with her?"

"This isn't *Mean Girls*. She was creeped out. So were a lot of us."

"Us?"

"I don't even know how many times I wake up every night thinking something's crawling on me."

Will hadn't known that part. He leaned against the wall next to her, wondering if he was supposed to pat her arm or something. It wasn't like he could hug her or anything—they were at *school*.

"Whatever," Hollie said, straightening. "It's just until I can be sure the crickets are all gone and this bug stuff blows over. Kathryn's baking the cookies until then."

"You can't give her the recipe!" It was like an evil volleyball plot to steal Hollie's famous cookies.

She rolled her eyes. "I found it online. I don't want the team to suffer because of my idiot brother."

"Gee, thanks."

"Just tell your idiot friends not to send any more bugs to the house."

Will huffed again, trying to think of a good comeback, but he was too slow, because for all her tough words, she walked away with her shoulders slumped—and he knew the extra weight on them was from him.

BY THURSDAY NIGHT AND THEIR FIRST WRESTLING MEET,
Will was ready to hit the mats and work out the wormy
nerves in his stomach. Practices were intense but couldn't
match the intensity of facing off with an opponent for real.

The grind of the season wouldn't get going until
December. Then one night a week they'd have a dual—a
meet against one other team—though sometimes it would
be a tri or quad against two or three teams, and every
Saturday they'd have a daylong tournament against a bunch
of teams from all over Minnesota. For now, though, they'd
have a tournament next weekend after Thanksgiving, and
tonight's warm-up meet.

It was at home, so the guys rolled out the good mats in
the main gym, then did some easy warm-ups, the other
team joining them after they sloughed off their winter
gear. It still hadn't snowed, though everyone was at that
point of wanting it to cover up all the dead and brittle and
gray and brown. Clean white snow that sparkled under a

blue sky, that Will could roll around in and sled down and snowmobile over—except Darryl was the one who had snowmobiles.

Thinking of Darryl made Will's stomach twist even more; he was already worried about Mr. Herrera. Eloy's dad would be there soon, the first contact Will would have with him since his post-science-presentation phone call. Will didn't like disappointing his parents, but they were used to it. Mr. Herrera was someone he maybe could have impressed—had wanted to impress.

Will *really* needed to wrestle.

Then he spotted Eloy. Though the gym walls were mostly cream-colored, the bleachers and the wall pads beneath the basketball hoops were school-color maroon. Eloy, in maroon track pants and a maroon Triton Cobras hoodie, blended in so well as to be nearly invisible.

"Hey," Will said.

Eloy squinted as if the lights were too bright. It kind of felt like they were.

They hadn't talked much since Monday, which was tough, since they'd had practice every afternoon as usual and, as usual, were paired up with each other. Most of Will's mad had burned off—it was hard to stay mad while working your guts out wrestling—but he wasn't looking forward to seeing Eloy's dad again, and that was a feeling he'd never thought he'd have.

"So, uh, is he here?" Will scanned the bleachers, but they

were mostly empty. With weigh-in at 4:00 P.M., most of the guys had simply stayed after school, but the meet didn't start until 5:00 P.M. Will's parents weren't there yet either.

Eloy shook his head.

"This sucks," Will moaned.

"He helped you," Eloy said through his teeth. "He deserves your respect."

"What?" Will blinked, then realized what his comment had sounded like. "Not that. The first time I met him, I was a sweaty mess, and then I had to call and apologize for the thing. I wanted to meet him the first time and, like, lay palm trees at his feet."

Eloy took a turn blinking.

"You know, like the Romans, and feeding each other grapes or whatever."

Eloy continued to blink.

"I saw it on TV!"

"Isn't your mom a teacher?" Eloy said.

"I know what I'm talking about," Will grumped.

"That's good, because no one else does." Eloy's face was a little too straight. When Will thumped his arm, Eloy cracked a smile and thumped him back.

Will leaned back against the wall beside Eloy, looking out at their teammates. A couple were in the bleachers, listening to music on their headphones to get into the zone. Most hung out on the mats, stretching, practicing moves in slo-mo, or simply lying down, eyes closed, though Will knew they weren't asleep. They were all pretty far away, closer to the basketball hoop opposite the one Eloy had staked out.

"What are you doing over here?" Will asked.

Eloy shrugged.

Will cleared his throat. "I do get that entomophagy stuff. It's, like, important. For the world."

Eloy sighed and pressed a fist to his chest. "It's something I feel in here. It's like a fist *in* my chest, around my heart. I don't really care about entomophagy, but the grasshoppers—I knew it would be fun, but I'm afraid they were a joke."

It was clear Eloy meant what he said, but Will just didn't get the worry because he didn't think they *were* a joke. "People ate them, and it wasn't terrible, and now maybe the idea isn't so freaky to them."

"Everyone's a bug-eater now—is that it?"

"Yeah?" He knew they *weren't,* in that people wouldn't repeat the experience anytime soon, but they *were* "bug-eaters," because they already had. At least that was a first step. "You know, you've probably helped save the world."

The contortions of Eloy's face expressed total skepticism . . . and maybe a little forgiveness.

Will grinned. "If you wrote down that heart stuff for language arts, Mrs. Olsen would fall all over herself to give you an A."

"Menso," Eloy said. Then after a bit, he added, "My dad would hate to hear that something he cooked was only 'not terrible.'"

Will sprang from the wall, scanning the bleachers too fast to actually see anything. "Omigosh, is he here?"

Eloy laughed in Will's face.

The refs called everyone together for weigh-in and groom check, scanning for skin diseases, too-long fingernails or bangs, or harsh beard stubble. The disappointing smoothness of Will's cheeks barely earned a glance, but Eloy's face got a good once-over. Eloy wasn't hairy, and he was actually shorter than Will, but the definition of his muscles and the squareness of his shape made him seem older, more manly. But he was fidgeting like a little kid. Eloy was nervous, too. Maybe a lot nervous, reminding Will that this was Eloy's first-ever wrestling match.

Since it was only the two teams, the brackets went up quickly. Will had expected it, but it was still pretty cool to see himself listed as the varsity wrestler in his weight class.

Eloy was in the same class, wrestling JV. He stared at the list, looking paler and paler.

"Dude," Will said, "it's going to be all right." Except then he glanced past Eloy and saw the Herreras arrive.

Will suspected he went pale, too. He whispered, "He's here."

Mr. Herrera carried Elsi on his back, smiling at something she was whispering into his ear, while Melanie, who was in third grade, carefully led a path up the bleachers.

"They look so happy," Will groaned. He didn't want to be the guy who spoiled Mr. Herrera's night. It didn't matter that Will had apologized over the phone; he needed to do it again in person.

Mrs. Herrera spotted Eloy and waved, but when she turned her gaze to Will, she frowned just like Will's mom did before she chewed him out.

"She totally hates me now."

"She doesn't hate you," Eloy said, watching his family march up the bleachers. "But I am glad she's not mad at *me*. If she switches to Spanish, you are *so* in trouble."

"Thanks for the support," Will muttered.

Eloy grinned and led the way to his family.

Will said a scratchy hi to Mrs. Herrera, Elsi, and Melanie, then held out his hand to shake Mr. Herrera's, though he was afraid. The man worked with *knives* all day. "Hello, sir," Will croaked, the back of his neck red-hot. "I'm sorry about what happened, and what you did was so amazing, and the *chap-oo-LEEN-ays* were so good, and you're awesome."

Mr. Herrera peered at him from beneath his eyebrows.

What the heck had Will done? Mr. Herrera was going to burn Will's food every time Will ate at the restaurant from now on—and Will would deserve it.

"Kids need to get into trouble every now and then," Mr. Herrera said, adding sharply, "But only a little, and only every now and then."

"Yes, sir," Will said.

Mrs. Herrera looked ready to take her turn with Will, and it clearly would *not* go as well as with Mr. Herrera, and Will knew he should let her, but he couldn't help blurting, "They were really good, and everyone tried one—I don't know if Eloy told you that—and a bunch of people ate a lot more than one. They were *gone* by the end of class! To make that happen? You're basically a wizard."

"Nerd," Eloy said.

Will thumped Eloy's arm.

"The two of you!" Mrs. Herrera said with such a pointed look at both of them, all four kids straightened up. At least she hadn't switched to Spanish yet.

Mr. Herrera grinned. "Maybe you should go back to your team now."

Will followed Eloy down the bleachers, relieved that Eloy's dad didn't seem too upset with him. "He can burn my food the rest of my *life*." As long as Mr. Herrera cooked it.

Eloy looked at Will funny, but he must have understood, because he grinned like his dad and clapped Will on the back.

26

WILL AND ELOY JOINED THE GUYS TO CHILL BEFORE THE
meet. Lying on their bellies, heads together in a circle, they
talked strategy and which guys to watch on the other team.
Trey and Kaleb got up to practice a few moves in slo-mo,
then monkeyed around, inspiring Will and Eloy to join
them. Somersaults. Cartwheels. At one point, Max and Trey
stretched Will between them by his hands and feet so he
hung like a hammock in the air.

After a while they all piled up, bellies turned into pil-
lows for one another. Trey crawled on top, lying on everyone indiscriminately of what body parts were where. The
guys pushed him around to get comfortable but didn't push
him off. They were an angular hodgepodge of bodies at
right angles but with goals and spirits aligned. Will was part
of something bigger in that moment. It filled him with the
courage he needed to face his opponent and bring pride to
his team.

Except just then, head propped on Randy's stomach, Will spotted Darryl in the bleachers. Darryl, who rarely came to Will's meets and who wasn't there with Simon.

Darryl, who didn't belong.

Will would have liked for Darryl to belong. He would have liked for everyone to get along already and have all this weirdness be over.

Spying Dad and Grandpa talking with Coach Van Beek, Will got up and headed over to say hi and waved at Mom, Hollie, Grandma, Pop-Pop, and Gran, who sat with the Herreras. Elsi had staked out a spot on Mom's lap, and Melanie was explaining something very seriously to Gran.

"Squash him like a bug, Bug Boy!" someone shouted from the bleachers.

"Sting him like a bee!"

Will flexed his muscles for the crowd, earning a few approving hoots and one "Eh, maybe the other guy will be a pipsqueak."

Will laughed at the joke with everyone else.

But Darryl didn't, and Will got that digging feeling in his gut again.

At quarter to five, the team headed to the locker room to get into their gear. As they pulled on their singlets, the guys were quiet, focused. It never took long to sling themselves into their uniforms. Most guys only pulled up the bottom half and would wait until just before the start of their bouts to loop the straps over their shoulders.

Will tugged his singlet on, then got back into his sweats to keep warm. Returning to the gym, he saw Darryl just staring at him.

They had been friends their whole lives; Will knew what it looked like when Darryl was up to something. But what?

Then Will's leg tickled. It almost felt like something was crawling on him. He scratched his leg, then felt the same thing on his side.

Up ahead, Eloy stopped so abruptly, Randy bumped into him. Eloy tugged at the bottom of his shorts. He jiggled his legs. Then he pulled his half-on, half-off uniform out at the waist to look inside.

Will didn't have to. When he lifted his sweatshirt, three black bugs were crawling up his belly.

He looked back up at his former best friend.

Darryl had put ants in their pants.

WILL AND ELOY HOLLERED AND JUMPED AROUND LIKE, well, they had ants in their pants.

Eloy hopped from foot to foot, smacking himself.

Will threw off his sweats and hooked his thumbs into his singlet, already pushing it down before Coach Van Beek grabbed his wrists, stopping him from stripping in the gym, in front of *everyone*. He didn't care enough to be embarrassed; there were *bugs* crawling on him.

Holding out the legs of his singlet, Will bounced, but it was pointless. The ants wouldn't be dislodged by his thrashings.

The guys were confused about what was happening until Will shouted, "Ants!" He dimly noticed that Darryl wasn't laughing. He only made sure Will saw him, and then he left the gym.

The team formed a protective circle around Will and Eloy, hustled them into the locker room, and tossed them into the shower so fast, the ants had barely moved.

Even as he rinsed off ants, Will couldn't believe it. Like, for *real*, could not believe one of his best friends would prank him like this. Not prank—Simon's box of crickets had been a prank—retaliate. This had been retaliation. Ants in their pants sounded funny but straight-up was *not*, not at all. It was mean. Will still felt the creepy tingle of the ants on his skin, the shower not so much washing away as echoing the icky sensation. Will slapped off the water.

Across from him, Eloy stood, head bowed, as if the water was too heavy on his neck for him to keep his head up.

"I'm sorry for getting you into the middle of this crap," Will said to him.

Eloy didn't say anything, but at least he looked up.

"It's just wrong," Will added.

Dad and Mr. Herrera were in the locker room now, too, talking with the coaches and refs. On another kind of day, Will knew his neck would heat up, that he'd be hot with embarrassment and anger. But right then he only felt cold, through and through.

The team from Goodhue was just as mad as Will's own. They were the first to suggest changing the order of the matches so Will and Eloy could go later and have time to regroup. But sitting in the bleachers, supporting his new teammates, Will didn't regroup. He dwelled upon what had happened.

Will and Eloy's opponents in particular made a point of

finding them to say that what had happened wasn't cool and to wish them a good match. Their integrity made Darryl's lack of it feel even sharper.

What kind of friend, even a ticked-off one, did something like this? It was as if Will had kicked sand at Darryl, and Darryl had retaliated with a grenade.

And all Will could think about now was how to drop an atomic bomb.

28

WILL AND ELOY LOST THEIR MATCHES.

Eloy made some good moves and scored a few points. He seemed pretty focused, considering.

Will wasn't.

Good wrestling was as much about brains as brawn, and his brain kept telling him there were ants in his singlet and showing him Darryl's face.

Tonight was Will's first match as a varsity wrestler. It was Eloy's first match, *ever.* Their families were there. Their coaches and team were watching.

Darryl knew what wrestling meant to Will, this year in particular. What he'd done was a kick in Will's face. Getting Eloy, too, was only a bonus for Darryl. He hadn't gone crazy because of "some Mexican." He'd lost it because Will hadn't gone along with him. Apparently in Darryl's world, friends weren't allowed to disagree with him or have different opinions about people.

After the meet, after the guys told them they'd done a good job and the coaches said they'd kept it together despite the circumstances, Will said to Eloy, "We're going to make Darryl pay."

Eloy finished putting on his shoes before looking up. "The coaches will take care of it."

"Are you crazy? I know Darryl. If we don't do something, he'll just keep at us, pulling crap like this all the time."

"What he did sucked, but you know *why* he did it."

Will wondered if his clenched jaw looked as square as Eloy's. "You're mad, too."

"Yes." He looked at the fists on his knees and unclenched them. "Yes, but like you said, you *know* Darryl. You're friends, and yet he could do something like this to you?"

"Oh, we're not friends anymore." Will slammed his gear into his duffel bag and wished he had a locker door to slam, too, but they only had cubbies. He gave one of the benches a kick, enjoying the squeal as it slid a few inches across the floor.

"Cool it," Randy said.

"Coach will take care of it," Max said.

They gave Will and Eloy thumps on the back as they headed out, most of the others on their way, too.

"Listen," Eloy said. "Guys like that *don't* listen, and they don't change. You just have to walk away. As much as I'd like to do something, it's pointless."

Will glared at Eloy. Walk away? What if Will had walked away when Darryl gave Eloy crap that day in the library? "None of this would have happened if I hadn't stood up for you, and now you're saying you won't stand up for me?"

"It's not like that."

"Whatever." Will slung his bag over his shoulder. Eloy wanted him to walk away. So he did. Alone.

29

"WHATEVER YOU WANT TO DO, I'M IN," SIMON SAID.

Simon's unquestioning loyalty was a sharp contrast to Eloy's and eased the tightness in Will's chest. *This* was what true friendship looked like.

For so long, it had been Will and Darryl and Simon. Without Darryl, Will had felt lopsided, like a three-legged stool missing a leg. Eloy had propped them up for a while, but he had shown his true colors tonight, as if everything Will had done for him didn't mean anything.

"I still can't believe he did it," Will admitted, not quite sure if he meant Darryl or Eloy.

"We can put turds in his locker, since he is one," Simon said.

Simon could always make Will smile. "I don't want to collect turds, do you?"

"Point taken."

Will's smile faded. "You heard about it fast." Word would

get around—Will never doubted that—but Simon had called only minutes after Will got home. Wrestling wasn't like football or basketball, which many people watched just because. Most who went to meets were related to a wrestler. Of course, that meant people from his class like Megan were there, since her brother was on the team. She wasn't the kind to spread rumors, but she might have texted Simon to give him a heads-up for Will's sake.

"Uh," Simon said.

Simon lost for words was a bad, bad sign.

"There's video."

Will closed his eyes. Of course there was video. Darryl hadn't stayed to record the mayhem he caused, but he wouldn't have had to. Someone always had a phone and a speedy trigger finger.

"Do you want me to send it to you?" Simon asked quietly. "So you can be prepared?"

"Might as well. Everyone else will have seen it."

"So, uh, what's the plan?"

"The plan? The plan is to make Darryl eat a bug if I have to shove it down his throat myself." His harsh breaths reverberated in the phone, making him hear how rabid he sounded. He blew the air from his lungs slowly and listened to how quiet Simon was.

Finally, Simon said, "I know you two are mad at each other, but . . . we're all still friends, right?"

Did Simon truly think this was something Will could get over? It felt as if that possibility had stopped occurring to Will eons ago. But Simon gave Will an idea.

"That's how we can play it." Darryl wasn't stupid. The last thing he'd do was eat anything Will or Simon tried to give him. Heck, if he was smart, he'd get a food taster for a while.

But. If he could be fooled into thinking Will was over it. *That* might be enough to trick Darryl into . . . what? That was the problem. Will didn't have anything to trick Darryl into yet.

"I might have something," Simon said.

Simon always could make Will smile.

The next morning, Darryl wasn't at his locker when he should have been, and the longer Will waited, the more antsy he got. People kept *looking* at him.

Clearly, they'd seen the video. So had Will.

The first part wasn't there, but there was still plenty to see.

The zoom was too far, the video fuzzy, but it was clearly Will. He looked small in his sweats and smaller out of them. On everyone else, the spandex fitted itself to the body underneath it, so an opponent had nothing to grab on to. On Will, there were pockets of air beneath the fabric over his bottom ribs and hip bones.

Plenty of room for ants to get around in.

His jumping looked like a cartoon temper tantrum.

Eloy did a lot of frantic slapping, too, but only at first. He'd gotten organized about brushing off ants much more quickly than Will had.

Eloy had friends at his old school in Rochester. They and some of his relatives had wanted to come to his first match, but he'd asked them to wait until he got a few under his belt. He'd said he was nervous enough without everyone he cared about watching.

Boy, did that turn out to be a good call. Unless the video got to them, which was likely. Someone always knew someone who knew someone.

Will didn't like it. It made him more determined to get back at Darryl, even if Eloy was out of the picture.

But first Darryl had to show.

Will looked down the hallway to the main doors, then heard behind him, at the eighth-grade end of the hall, a yelp, a thud, and his sister's voice.

"Don't you dare talk to me like that again!"

Whatever had happened had happened too fast for a circle to form around her. Will dashed as quickly as he could to beat the crowd before it closed in. Because Hollie was in trouble. A guy was on the floor, holding his bloody nose, while Amy shrieked and Kathryn stared, openmouthed.

The guy on the ground was Jeremy, one of the football

players, short but fast. Though apparently not fast enough. "You hit me in the nose!" He sounded like he had a terrible cold, but it wasn't snot clogging his words.

Hollie stood over him, hands on her hips, not sorry *at all*. "That was an accident, and you know it, but what you did was on purpose, and never, ever talk to me or any other girl like that again."

"I didn't mean it the way it sounded!"

"How the heck does that make it better?"

"I'm sorry, Hollie! Really, I didn't mean it."

Hollie bloodied a guy's nose and got *him* to apologize to *her*? She was hard-core. The guys would welcome her to the wrestling team like a heavyweight, but what the heck had happened?

Before Will had a chance to step in and help—not that Hollie needed any—teachers were in the hall, lifting Jeremy and walking him and Hollie to the office.

He tried to get in front of them, to slow them down and give Hollie time to build a defense. But she gave him a look, as if his nose was next if he didn't get out of her way, and he had the terrible and certain feeling that he and his bugs had started it, whatever it was.

He darted back toward the eighth graders, hearing bits and pieces, before snagging Kathryn on her way to the office to be Hollie's witness.

Hollie had been putting something on the top shelf of her locker, when Jeremy sneaked up behind her and brushed her back, saying something about "ants in her pants." He'd surprised her, and when she jerked around, her elbow cracked his nose.

The elbow was a powerful force. Will knew from wrestling it was one of the strongest points on the body, and though he could use his elbows to maneuver and stuff in a match, he was not allowed to "elbow" opponents and definitely not allowed to crack them in the head.

Though he wouldn't have minded whacking Jeremy. It was one thing to put ants in a guy's pants, but a guy talking about ants in Will's *sister's* pants? It made him feel that there were ants crawling all over him again. Or, worse, that he was buried up to his neck in sand, and ants were being poured on his head.

Hollie shouldn't have to deal with crap like that, even if she obviously could.

Darryl had to pay.

But he still wasn't there. Will found out why when class started.

Darryl was forced to apologize to the wrestling team and the entire school over the PA system, though to Will he didn't sound sorry. He was clearly reading from something, and though Will knew Principal Raymond would have made Darryl write it himself, it sounded like a list of things he'd been told to say.

And a little like bragging.

It made people glance at Will and Eloy—not that anyone

needed prodding—and tuck in smiles, unable to pretend they were sorry about the most exciting weeks they'd ever had at school. Darryl's "apology" might as well have ended, "Don't forget to check out the video!"

Hollie, the looks, the fake apology—it was all terrible and just what Will needed to get himself ready. Because the hardest part of his plan wasn't getting Darryl to eat the bug, it was how Will was going to have to act.

He had to be Darryl's friend again.

30

WHEN DARRYL WALKED INTO CLASS, THE ONLY FREE SEAT was his old one between Will and Simon.

Darryl halted in the doorway, but Simon waved him over like a bored air traffic controller. Will suppressed the urge to leap over desks and get Darryl in a half nelson, instead making a show of rolling his eyes as if Darryl was nervous over nothing.

Mr. Hanson prodded Darryl to get a move on. Darryl sat as if the seat had a bomb strapped beneath it.

"Dude," Simon whispered to him. "Your prank is going down in history. Even Diggy Lawson hasn't pulled anything that good. Ants in the pants!" He overdid the laugh, but it was still convincing, since Simon generally overdid things.

Darryl peered at Simon, then glanced at Will before staring straight ahead again.

He wasn't buying it.

Will wouldn't have either. He had planned what to say but thought it would be before class. Having to sit through social studies first, having to sit next to Darryl through social studies and not think about Hollie getting hassled and not notice, too, how Eloy stared straight ahead, very purposeful in not looking their way . . . every muscle in Will's body was tense, braced for a takedown.

Will knew who Darryl really was now and looked forward to making him pay.

But Will didn't like how things looked to Eloy—or Cristian and Tyler—right now.

Eloy was his teammate and had been pretty decent about the crap Will had gotten him into. If Eloy had just listened and gone along with Will, he'd know things weren't how they seemed. He wouldn't think Will was the kind of jerk who would still be friends with someone who thought it was okay to call guys like Eloy names and humiliate him so publicly and in front of his family.

Will watched the clock so hard, he hypnotized himself. He didn't realize class had ended until Darryl was standing over him.

"So, what's the deal?" Darryl said. "You team up with that guy to give me a hard time with another bug in class, I repay the favor, and now we're square? You're saving me seats?" Though his disbelief was strong, he had sat with them when he could have gotten someone to switch, which meant something.

"The class presentation was *homework*, not a plot," Will said with another eye roll, as if Darryl was a drama queen for getting so bent out of shape over it—which he was. Will hadn't *teamed up* with Eloy because of Darryl. Bug Boy was bigger than Darryl—and even Will.

Though Darryl might have been a little right about Will giving him a hard time in class. At least Darryl didn't call Eloy "the Mexican" again, like it was an insult to be from Mexico. It was just a *place*.

Thinking about that helped Will go on. "And, yeah, I'm ticked about the ants, but I watched the video, and there's probably something wrong with me, but I couldn't help laughing." Will had practiced—a lot—so he could say that part without choking, and he didn't dare look, but he hoped Eloy was gone and hadn't heard what he'd just said.

He gathered his stuff and headed for their lockers like everything was normal, fingers crossed that Darryl would come along.

He did, though he lagged behind, intentionally, as if he didn't want to turn his back on Will or Simon.

"Remember when we soaped those ants for your grandma?" Will said. It was summer, before fourth or fifth grade. Cornfield ants had made mounds around her garden and apple trees. He and Darryl had poured buckets of soapy water onto them but had gotten too close. Ants had bitten their feet and legs. They'd rinsed off, then gotten into a water war, hoses and soapy buckets their weapons. It had been fun. Hanging out with *that* Darryl had always been fun.

Darryl didn't smile, but he kind of looked like he wanted to. "So you're saying we're cool?"

Will could not say that, even to make his plan work. "How long have we been friends?"

"Forever," Simon said, stretching the word into twice as many syllables.

Darryl looked down. "I didn't take that video," he said quietly. "I don't know who did."

It might have been an apology, a real one this time, and Will felt a twinge, as if maybe tricking Darryl wasn't a good idea. But then Darryl turned and looked right at Eloy, who was only a few lockers away. Close enough to hear enough. His red ears were proof.

Will probably should have been embarrassed, but all he felt was irritated. Eloy could have been in on the whole thing and known the truth about what was going down. He didn't have to, like, get his feelings hurt or whatever.

Though the truth was shifting. Will kind of didn't want to do this anymore. He wanted payback, but he also just felt mean.

"Oh, hey, Will," Simon said, playing too casual, "I brought something for you."

He handed Will a Ziploc bag of something that looked like old, cut-up bootlaces, leathery and gray.

Will tore into them like they were the best thing ever.

And very quickly realized he should have tried one beforehand.

Earthworm jerky was tougher than it looked.

AFTER THE *CHAPULINES* HAD BEEN SUCH A HIT, SIMON had gone on a bug-eater shopping spree with his dad's credit card. This time his dad *did* call to "chew" him out, a phrase Simon used repeatedly in telling the story.

Canned tarantula, chocolate-covered scorpion, dung beetles, giant centipede . . . and earthworm jerky. All edible. Supposedly.

Last night when Will had been stumped about how to get back at Darryl, Simon revealed what he had bought as Christmas gifts for Will, though they both knew he never could have held out that long. Canned tarantula and *dung* beetles? Will was only surprised Simon hadn't given him the "gifts" the day they arrived. Though it would be awesome to see Darryl eat a scorpion or dung beetle, they both agreed that the earthworm was probably the only thing they could get away with.

"You know Will," Simon told Darryl. "Always trying to

put on weight. I found snake jerky and had to get some. 'Cause we're the Triton *Cobras*, get it?"

The jerky did look a lot like snake skin, except for the part with the raised band that encircled the earthworm's body. He couldn't remember the name of that part but did remember it was where eggs were deposited. Most of the pieces looked like ordinary jerky, but that one looked like the flattened head of an earthworm that it was. Will was glad he hadn't grabbed it, and not only because it would have given them away to Darryl.

The jerky Will bit into was fighting back.

His teeth practically came out of his head when he tried to tear off a chunk. He had to saw at it, grinding his teeth back and forth.

"There's a reason they make boots out of snakeskin," Simon said extra cheerily. "You should try some," he said to Darryl. "How cool to say we ate snake." Then he took a strip of earthworm from the bag, though he hesitated before eating it himself, watching Will's contortions.

When the piece finally ripped free, it slid partway under Will's tongue. Saliva gathered around it, taking a crack at softening it. Will had to swallow the growing pool of spit and tasted spicy spices, like cayenne and chili powder, and plenty of salt like in regular jerky.

Slightly reassured, he gave it a chew.

And chewed. And chewed. Earthworm was *tough*.

And sandy.

The grit in his teeth was like fingernails on a chalkboard. It made his spine vibrate. Then things got worse.

Because Will had chewed away the spices and the salt. All that was left was earthworm.

Earthworm tasted like old, rotted fish skin.

Will's gag reflex kicked in. He suppressed it, but there was no way he'd be able to swallow the vile thing in his mouth. *No. Way.* He wanted it out *now*.

He gagged again, jaw contracting in that classic—and visible—pre-puke motion. If he didn't get it out now, he was going to throw up, again, but Darryl was standing there watching, and though Will didn't care anymore about his stupid plan to get Darryl to eat a bug, he also didn't want Darryl to figure out it was a trick.

If he could just swallow, it would be over with, but he couldn't. More saliva pooled in his mouth, a lake of rancid, fishy spit.

"That's not snake, is it?" Darryl said. He grabbed the Ziploc bag and pulled out the largest piece, the one with the raised band around the body, the one that *looked* like what it was—a giant earthworm.

"We're eating it, aren't we?" Simon said, though he hadn't put his piece of jerky anywhere near his mouth.

It was supportive of Simon to try to keep the ploy alive or at least secret, but Will was *relieved* to be caught. He spit the wad of worm into his hand and desperately scanned the hall, pre-puke panic clouding his brain about where the nearest fountain was so he could wash the nauseating taste from his mouth.

But before he could bolt for water and deliverance from the putrid flavors, Darryl crowded him into the lockers. "You two teamed up against me for another bug thing? Is that all you care about now?" His voice cracked.

The wash of guilt Will felt wasn't fair.

"You put ants in our pants," he said. Last night, that was all the reason he'd needed. Now, after time to cool down, with Darryl's angry hurt in Will's face, he didn't feel like he'd balanced the scales of justice. He felt like a jerk.

Darryl had gone way over the top with those ants, just like he had when Eloy called him crazy in the library, when it *had* been crazy to almost smash all those stinkbugs. Darryl never had a sense of scale.

But Will did.

He knew better. An eye for an eye only leveled the field if you wanted a dust bowl.

But Darryl had put *ants* in Will's *pants*. Video had gone around the *entire school*. Hollie had been teased and had *drawn blood* because of it. It wasn't fair for Will to feel bad now, for *Darryl*. Darryl hadn't even eaten the stupid worm! Will was the one suffering. Again.

He shoved Darryl, clearing room to get his back off the lockers. No wrestling technique, just raw anger.

"You want me to eat a bug?" Darryl said. "Fine." He

tossed the entire chunk of earthworm jerky into his mouth, then opened wide, showing it off to Will, Simon—and Eloy.

Will's stomach turned over. Sharp and too bright, the memory came to him of the conversation he'd had with Eloy before barely any of this had begun, when Will had needed Mr. Herrera's help with the *chapulines*. Eloy had been nervous. He'd said there was a difference between being funny and a joke and asked straight up if it *was* all a joke.

Darryl doing "see food" with the earthworm made it one.

He spit it onto the floor. "We're even," he said, and Will got that he meant a bug for a bug, though Darryl still hadn't technically eaten one. It didn't matter. He didn't have to. He shouldered past Will and walked away.

Simon fiddled with the Ziploc bag of earthworm jerky, lining up the red and blue strips as if the fate of the color purple depended on it. "That was," he said slowly, "not what I expected."

"Who the heck does he think he is?" Will kicked a locker. He would *not* feel bad about Darryl. Not after everything that had happened. Not after what *Darryl* had started that day in the library. They weren't even. Not even close. Because Darryl kept starting crap—and kept getting away with it.

Will tried doing *one* thing—one thing that didn't even work—and somehow *he* was the jerk? No one had said it, but Will felt it in the eyes that looked at him. And especially the eyes that didn't: Simon's.

"I think, uh," Simon said, "we might have hurt his feelings."

Will wasn't sure he cared about Darryl's feelings, but he did care about Simon's. "I'm sorry I got you involved." Simon had always been in the middle, but he wouldn't be anymore. Will had messed up Simon and Darryl's friendship almost as bad as Will and Darryl's. But Will was afraid it was worse than that and kicked a locker again. Because Will hadn't only pulled Simon to his side, he'd essentially created a gang: He'd pitted both of Darryl's best friends against him.

Will looked at the gob of chewed, spit-slimy earthworm still in his hand and worried that the only real worm there was him.

ELOY WALKED OVER, STARING AT THE PLASTIC BAG'S
contents.

"I don't want to hear it," Will grumbled. "You already said it last night." Eloy might have been right about Will needing to cool down, but it wasn't like he could just decide to cool down and that would make it happen. The back of his neck, his ears, his face, the center of his chest—everything felt like it was on fire.

Eloy's jaw was square, but Will didn't need that clue to know that Eloy was mad. "Your 'payback' was tricking him into eating a bug? Because people who eat bugs are too stupid to know any better, right?" he said, quoting what Darryl had said during the science presentation.

"No!" Jeez. Leave it to Eloy to make it sound worse than it was. "He hadn't eaten one yet," Will explained. "That's all it was."

"I thought you got it," Eloy said. "I thought you weren't

just using something that means something to my dad to get a laugh."

"That isn't how it was! I've been on your side this whole time. I've helped you."

Eloy took a step back, but it wasn't in retreat. He stood tall and stared at Will, not like a glare, more like an examination. As if Will were a bug he couldn't quite identify.

Eloy not saying anything left Will's last words ringing in his ears. Had he been on Eloy's side? Had he "helped" him? Because Will had a bad feeling that maybe he hadn't. That maybe he'd thought he'd done Eloy a favor and that Eloy owed him. For what? For not being cool with someone—not only someone, his *best friend*—calling a kid a *cholo* and "the Mexican" as if they were dirty words? That wasn't doing Eloy a favor. That was being a decent person. Eloy didn't owe Will anything for acting the way any decent person should. Will hadn't really thought that, had he?

"Worms aren't actually bugs," he mumbled.

"Huh?" Eloy said.

"Worms aren't insects. They're, like, their own phylum or something."

"I don't care *what* bug it is. You might as well have made fun of my dad right to his face."

That rotted, fishy taste still coated Will's mouth. "I wouldn't." He swore it. "I love your dad."

"You don't know anything about him. You just like his

food. You'd say you love Ben and Jerry and Little Debbie, too."

That wasn't true. He could see Mr. Herrera in his mind, stopping by their table at El Corazón and laughing at Will's outrageous compliments. Could see him at the wrestling meet, letting Will off the hook so easily. It wasn't true, because Will did know something about Mr. Herrera that he didn't about Ben, Jerry, or Little Debbie. "I know he's my friend's dad."

Eloy slumped. He stared again at the clear Ziploc bag Simon still held. "You used it for payback. Like eating a bug is *punishment*."

He walked away, off to the same class all of them had to get to—Darryl, Eloy, Simon, and Will. The hallway was nearly empty. Simon gave Will the earthworms and patted him on the back before leaving Will behind, sensing he needed a minute on his own.

He did. He thought about Eloy holding a hand to his chest, trying to explain what he felt inside, like a fist squeezing his heart. All along, Will had wanted Eloy to be part of *Will's* team, but Eloy had been trying to make him see the other team, *their* team.

Too late, Will thought he got it.

Eating grasshoppers wasn't exactly part of Eloy's day-to-day life, but it wasn't weird, either. It was even ordinary when he visited his family in Mexico. But Will had treated it like it *was* weird and worse than weird, a trick to get back at someone.

Eloy had put up with Will a lot longer than Will would have if the situation were reversed. The only person who had done anyone a favor was Eloy. He'd given Will the benefit of the doubt, trying to make him see.

Will saw it now.

He thought *Darryl* had acted like a jerk to Eloy? Then what did that make Will? He had acted like he was a good guy for being friends with Eloy even though he was different. Like being different was weird.

If Will could turn into a bug, he'd let himself get squashed.

33

AFTER A DAY OF FEELING LIKE CRAP, IT WAS EASY FOR WILL to convince Coach Van Beek he *really* felt like crap and needed to skip wrestling practice. Will didn't have it in him to give Eloy any resistance. He'd spend the entire time pinned, and Eloy and the coaches would spend the entire time frustrated with him.

So he went home, to the waiting legs of dozens of crickets, their chirps hitting his ears like tiny cattle prods.

He wanted to fix things, but the thing to fix was him. How could he prove anything like that to Eloy?

Thinking of Eloy made Will think about Darryl. The thing was, Will wasn't sure he wanted to fix things with Darryl. He wasn't okay ignoring the stuff that had been said—that felt the same as saying it himself—and he couldn't stop hearing Darryl say "Mexican" as if it were a curse word. Will could get over the ants, but he had a feeling in his chest, like Eloy had said: a fist around his heart. Will had to square things with Eloy first.

Eloy thought Will had eaten and served bugs as a joke, for entertainment, as punishment. He was right.

So to show he understood how wrong he was, Will had to eat bugs for real, like he meant it.

And the truth was, he did mean it. All that stuff he'd said during his class presentation was true. Entomophagy only seemed freaky because bugs were *bugs*. He'd struck out with raw stinkbug and earthworm jerky, but he didn't like cucumbers, cream cheese, or eggplant either. The *chapulines* had been good, and other insects could be, too.

But he could eat them like he meant it, alone, all he wanted, and that wouldn't prove anything to Eloy or anyone else. He had to get other people interested in eating bugs, too.

Sure, he'd gotten some people to eat grasshoppers— once, and basically on a dare. The number of grasshoppers that had been scattered underfoot in the hall was proof the interest in entomophagy went only so far and not beyond the door of Mr. Taylor's classroom.

Simon's online shopping spree was more proof. He didn't buy dung beetles and a canned tarantula because he seriously thought they'd be a nice snack.

But Simon *had* ordered them, something that wouldn't

have occurred to him a few weeks ago. That was a start, though a start to what, Will wasn't sure. He needed another plan.

And he needed to apologize—to a long list of people that he worried got longer by the minute.

He slumped low on the sofa, expecting the next few days to suck, and was oddly comforted when a cricket crawled from between the cushions onto his knee. Not quite Jiminy, but nice.

It sprang away when Hollie pushed open the front door.

She didn't look much better than he did. He was surprised when she let her bag slide to the floor and slumped onto the couch beside him.

"Um, are you okay?" he asked.

She leaned her head back, eyes closed. "I can't play in the next game."

"What?"

"I gave Jeremy a bloody nose."

"It was an accident."

"But I wasn't all that sorry."

"He brought it on himself."

"Yeah, well I can't play, and they don't want me in the concession stand, and I'm just really ready for you to be done with all this bug stuff," she said, eyes still closed and head leaned back as if she was too tired to even look at him.

"Um," he said again, abruptly *un*-tiring her.

She frowned directly at him. "What now?"

"I was thinking I needed to double down." He explained what Eloy had said, what it had made Will think about himself and the bugs, and what he'd thought he should do next. Laying it all out, the good, the bad, and the stupid, could have been embarrassing, but since Hollie had lived with him his whole life, the spectrum on Hollie's chart of Will's embarrassing moments was broad, like, spanned miles broad. By the end, Will felt a hundred pounds lighter, which would be bad for wrestling but was good for his heart.

"Hmm," Hollie said. "You might be growing up, little brother."

He rolled his eyes. "We're practically the same age."

She snorted. "You're a boy, so your maturity level is about four years behind mine, like dog years."

"Ha-ha. Hey, there's a cricket crawling up your ponytail."

It took Hollie less than three seconds to figure out Will was tricking her, but by then she had whipped her head around, the ponytail looping around her neck. "So I guess you don't want my help."

If Hollie had a plan for what to do next, he'd owe her for the rest of his *life*. Not that he'd tell her that. He cleared his throat. "Uh, do you have an idea?"

She only ran a hand down her ponytail.

"I'm sorry, I'm sorry, I'm sorry," he said as quickly as his mouth could keep up.

"You have a tournament coming up, right?" she asked.

His hopes dimmed. He did, but it was more than a week away, too long to leave things hanging. "Not until *next* Saturday, after Thanksgiving."

"Perfect," Hollie said.

Will looked at her. Did she really have a plan? Because the mere *thought* she did loosened the knot in his gut, and if she was messing with him . . .

"But you'll need Mr. Herrera's help," she added, briefly describing the beginning of her idea.

The knot tightened up again. Mr. Herrera had forgiven Will once and far too easily in Will's opinion, but a lot had happened since then, and who knew what Eloy had told his dad.

But both Eloy and Mr. Herrera had been on Will's apology list before Hollie mentioned anything about their help. He'd be talking with them whether or not he had a way to prove he was sorry. Though he didn't like the idea of saying "I'm sorry" and "Can you help me?" at the same time, it was better than a plain old sorry with nothing to back it up.

Will took a deep breath. "I'll see if Dad can give me a ride."

WILL FOUND DAD IN THE GARAGE, TINKERING WITH THE
snowblower.

"Is it supposed to snow?" Will asked. They still hadn't
had any, but it could start any day now.

"No predictions yet, but I wanted to be sure the three of
you would be okay if I was caught at the wrong end of the
tracks." Dad was good about stuff like that, thinking ahead
to make sure Mom, Hollie, and Will were prepared if he got
stuck on a train too long. Will could have used some of that
thinking-ahead experience before, but now he didn't want
it. He didn't want to think ahead to what Eloy would do
when Will knocked on his door.

"Will you take me to Eloy's?"

Dad squinted at him. "You feeling better?"

"Huh?" Then Will remembered. He'd claimed sickness to
skip wrestling practice. "Uh . . ."

"I wondered," Dad said. "Those ants would have rattled

anybody. But I hope you won't let it keep you from going back."

"Huh?" Will said again, genuinely confused. Then it hit him. The ants in the pants had happened only last night. It felt as if so many other things had happened since then, he'd practically forgotten about the ants. Did Coach think that's why Will had wanted out of practice? Because he was too embarrassed to get back on the mat? "Dad, I swear, that's not it at all."

"That was a pretty big stunt for Darryl to pull. Do you want to talk about what's going on with him?"

Will kind of shrugged. What was there to say? Darryl was different now. Or maybe he wasn't; maybe *Will* was different.

"Sometimes," Dad said, "people outgrow each other. It doesn't mean we stop caring or forget the good times, but maybe we realize we need different things, things we can't get from each other anymore."

Will wasn't quite sure what it was he needed that Darryl didn't have, but he got what Dad meant. Will and Darryl and Simon were getting older, and they *were* changing. Will didn't want to *just* change though. He wanted to have some choice, to think about who he *wanted* to be. He liked how Eloy had pushed him—accidentally or not—to think differently. He liked being Bug Boy, too. Not only because Bug Boy was cool, but also because Bug Boy got people to think differently, too, to try things they never thought they would. At least, he had once. He was determined to do it again.

"Thanks, Dad. I think for now I just need to talk to Eloy."

Dad nodded and went inside for the keys and to let Mom know where they were going. His agreement loosened something in Will's chest—and tightened something in his gut.

Will might need to talk to Eloy. But that didn't mean Eloy would talk to Will.

The ride over was quiet, Dad leaving Will to his thoughts, Will trying to organize them. Hollie's idea sounded cool, but so had everything else he'd done lately. He didn't exactly trust his judgment when it came to bug-related things.

At the door, Eloy's little sister, Elsi, answered again, their mom right behind scolding her again.

"Hi, Mrs. Herrera, Elsi. Is Eloy—?" His brain short-circuited before he could ask if Eloy was home. All mental resources were assigned to his nose. Someone was cooking, and it smelled amazing. "Omigosh, is Mr. Herrera cooking?"

Mrs. Herrera smiled. "Not here. Friday night he's too busy at the restaurant."

Will sniffed the air. It smelled so good, not like at El Corazón, but good.

"I made spaghetti sauce," she said, jolting Will, though it took him a second to figure out why.

She wasn't cooking Mexican food.

He wanted to kick his own butt. When would he stop

assuming stuff just because Eloy's family was Hispanic? Mrs. Herrera had said she was born in Minnesota—just like Will's mom. And even if she weren't, anyone from anywhere could make spaghetti sauce or macaroni and cheese or hamburgers or pizza or anything.

Will wanted to stay mad at himself, but he kept getting distracted. What he was smelling wasn't like any spaghetti sauce Will was used to. The scents were tangy and crisp, light. He thought of red sauce as heavy and meaty, but Mrs. Herrera's smelled . . . bright.

"The secret's in the olives and plenty of good white wine," she said, smiling at Will. "Would you two like to stay for dinner?"

"Heck, yeah," Dad said, walking right in as if it was nothing, already chatting with Eloy's mom and little sisters.

Will stayed at the door. It didn't seem right to just walk in, not without Eloy saying it was OK.

He obviously hadn't said anything to his mom about what had happened that morning. She looked back at Will, stuck at the door, and pointed down a hallway. "He's in the laundry room, cleaning his gear."

That's where Will cleaned his stuff, too, and that little bit of connection was enough to move his feet. The hall wasn't long. He saw Eloy as soon as he rounded the corner and realized Eloy had to have heard Will arrive. And hadn't come out.

He cleared his throat. "Hey."

Eloy had a container of bleach wipes and used the tops of the washer and dryer as a work surface, just like Will did. He was careful to hit every part of his headgear, then set it upside down to air dry.

"Um, your mom invited us to stay for dinner." That wasn't what he'd meant to say first! The problem was, he didn't really know what to say, even though he'd tried to think ahead.

Eloy crossed his arms and finally looked at him. "What do you want?" He didn't say it meanly exactly, but Will got the point that he wasn't getting any help with saying what he needed to say.

He took a deep breath. "I'm sorry for using you for grasshoppers."

Eloy peered at Will as if he'd grown a giant zit on his forehead.

"It was wrong, because treating something normal for you like it's weird is as bad as calling you names."

Eloy rolled his eyes as if Will were being melodramatic. Will wanted to grab Eloy's shoulders and make him pay better attention. Will was serious.

"In the future, I'll be more respectful of you and your culture."

"Jeez, Will, it wasn't that bad."

Will blinked. "Yes, it was."

Eloy shook his head. "You were being a bonehead, and, yeah, I was mad, and it would be nice if I didn't have to call you on it every time you're a bonehead. You know, if you could figure it out yourself."

"That I'm a bonehead?"

"Yeah." Eloy kind of grinned but then didn't. He said quietly, "Do you know how hard it is to be Mexican in Minnesota? You're all so *white*."

They were all so white. Will had never really thought about it until becoming friends with Eloy. But the guys on the team and a bunch of kids at school, both Hispanic and white, were friends with Eloy, real friends. Like Will. "People like you, Eloy."

"Most of them didn't try to get to know me until you decided I was okay. Before that, I was the new kid, and a Mexican, too."

"You are the new kid."

"And Mexican."

Will looked down the hall into the living room that had surprised him the first time he visited. By how ordinary it was, ordinary for a guy from Minnesota who sometimes visited Mexico. "I don't think people care, exactly."

"Some do. You know they do," Eloy said meaningfully, and Will knew he meant Darryl.

"Yeah," Will sighed. "But, I think for other people, they're just not familiar with it, you know? You speak Spanish at school, and no one says anything."

"I didn't used to speak Spanish at school, even with my

friends in Rochester. But then you got all excited when I cursed at practice."

Will remembered that practice. Eloy had found the loophole about cursing. "So you started speaking Spanish more because of me?"

Eloy rolled his eyes.

Will puffed up. "See? I'm a good guy. I've been *telling* you."

"You're a *menso* who sometimes, accidentally, steps into doing something kind of okay."

"You say that like it doesn't count."

Eloy laughed. "See? *Menso.* I've been telling you."

Will felt like he'd dropped a ton of weight again. Eloy probably should have been madder at Will, but it wasn't his style, and Will was grateful. He thought about putting him in a headlock but then remembered something Eloy had said once.

He stepped forward and hugged Eloy.

"What are you doing?" Eloy asked, not moving.

"I remember you saying some men just hug each other." Will added a couple claps on the back before stepping away. "So I hugged you."

"Ah."

Will squinted at Eloy's too-straight face.

"You know how you tell this is Minnesota?" Eloy asked. He put Will in a headlock.

Will, smelling armpit, fake gagged like he was face-first in toxic waste. "Deodorant is your friend."

"No, it's *your* friend," Eloy said.

"So you'll help me?" Will said.

"Que Dios me ayude."

"That sounded like, 'Yes, absolutely, I can't wait, because I'm sure your idea is genius and you are a genius and the best wrestler and also very handsome.'"

"When you're finished 'translating,' you can actually ask me whatever it is you need help with. And eat spaghetti."

Being put in a headlock was the easiest apology Will had ever given. And his escape was a technical masterpiece. Herrera cooking was on the line, after all.

35

THE PLAN WAS A BUCK-A-BUG FUND-RAISER.

It was the kind of idea that would either be mind-blowingly amazing—or that would completely, utterly tank.

Hollie figured few would eat a bug just because, but many might if it were for a good cause. Will loved wrestling but didn't think a fund-raiser for the team would be enough to get people out, so they agreed to raise funds for cancer research in honor of one of their teachers, Mrs. Graf, who had died a few years earlier.

While working on his science presentation, Will had found all sorts of recipes for different bug dishes. At the time, they'd just seemed funny: Bugs in a Rug, Really Hoppin' John, Scorpion Scaloppine. Now he got that the names *were* funny, not to make fun of eating bugs but to be inviting, to encourage people to think of insect dishes as not scary but a welcome change from the ordinary.

As long as they did, for real, taste good.

That's where Mr. Herrera came in.

While food preparation would happen behind the scenes, Will would officially come out as a bug eater at school. He talked with Coach Van Beek and Mr. Taylor first, partly because the plan wouldn't happen without them, but also because he respected them and knew his antics had affected them, too. Getting their agreement, Will then went public via the school's PA system.

The pages of his speech were crumpled from too much handling in his sweaty hands. By the time the bells rang and Principal Raymond signaled him to start, his heart pounded like he'd done a thousand sprints.

He cleared his throat—into the mic—and heard feedback echo in the hall.

"My fellow Cobras, I am Will Nolan."

Classrooms erupted with so much noise, Will could hear it from inside the office. He hoped the loud reaction was a good thing. He cleared his throat again, into the mic, again, which made the principal and secretary wince again—and the classrooms abruptly go silent.

"I'm Will Nolan, and I'm an entomophagist," he said, concentrating to say it correctly: *en-toe-MOFF-ah-jist.* "That means I eat bugs. On purpose." Another wave of sound rolled down the hallway, bolstering him for the next part. "I'm here today to announce the Buck-a-Bug fund-raiser for cancer research. For every dollar donated, you, too, can eat a delicious bug."

This time, the only sound in the hall was a cricket chirp.

"Mr. Herrera, chef at the famous El Corazón, will prepare several treats to tempt your taste buds. And, if we raise two hundred fifty dollars, I will publicly eat an entire scorpion."

The roar from the classrooms rattled windows.

When Hollie had suggested the scorpion challenge, Will had protested, because it seemed like using insects as punishment again, and also because she'd said *scorpion*. He argued that scorpions were part of the arachnid class, not insects, but Hollie didn't care about technicalities. She wanted him to eat one. From the reactions outside the principal's office, so did everyone else.

Eloy had been cool with the idea, noting that the extra incentive would likely get more people in the door. But Will was pretty sure, in this case, that Eloy was also cool with the idea of the scorpion as a bit of a punishment.

Will tried to keep his focus on the raising $250 part.

"The Buck-a-Bug fund-raiser will begin at noon outside the gym this Saturday. I hope you will join me by coming early and staying late to support our wrestling team at our first tournament. My fellow wrestlers at Triton are some of the most honorable, hardest-working people I've ever met, and they represent our school with pride every time they step onto the mat." Will blinked fast and swallowed, and it was so weirdly quiet, he feared everyone heard the gulp. He hadn't been a great representative of the team so far, and the guys deserved serious respect.

"So bring your dollars and come to the Buck-a-Bug fundraiser Saturday at noon. We've ordered all kinds of yummy bugs and the scorpion. And I'm willing to share."

When he turned off the mic, Principal Raymond patted his back. Will wiped his forehead. He hadn't realized he was sweating, and he had to do this two more times, at the high school and the elementary school. But his school was the one he cared about most, and he had all limbs crossed that the plan would work.

BECAUSE IT WASN'T FAIR FOR MR. HERRERA TO HAVE TO
do all the cooking, Will had talked with Mom and Dad and
placed a special order first thing Monday morning. One recipe had stuck in his mind, one he thought he and the guys
could make, but his confidence wavered when the shipment
arrived.

Wax worms. Five hundred in two blue containers of
sawdust.

Alive.

Will watched them for a while, gently tilting the
thin plastic cups to reveal the chunky, wriggling baby
caterpillars before they burrowed back into the wood
shavings. They were kind of creepy, because they looked
like maggots. But they also were small, pale, and seemed so
defenseless trying to dig under cover.

He sent some video of the squirming worms to Eloy and
Simon, to give them time to back out from helping him if
they wanted. Eloy called right away.

"You don't have to do it. My dad said he doesn't mind."

"I haven't cooked any of the bugs I've eaten yet. If I'm going to call myself an entomophagist, I need to learn. Uh, right?" He may have tacked on the last part in case Eloy wanted to talk him out of it—but Eloy didn't.

Simon only texted: *DUUUUUUUUUUUDE!!!!!*

Will put the wax worms into the freezer and turned the temp as low as it would go so they wouldn't suffer.

Thanksgiving was always chaotic, because both sets of grandparents cooked, so Will had lunch in town with Grandma and Grandpa and all his aunts, uncles, and cousins on Mom's side, then dinner in Faribault with Gran and Pop-Pop and all his aunts, uncles, and cousins on Dad's side. But this year the chaos escalated to mayhem, because everyone knew everything about Will and "his" bugs. It was disturbing to find out that some people in schools his cousins went to had seen the video and heard stories about Will, but it was balanced by the fact that a bunch of his relatives who didn't live too far out promised to come to the fund-raiser. His cousins might be making all sorts of ridiculous jokes now, but Will was pretty sure they'd be there for him when the time came. Like eighty percent sure, judging by how some couldn't stop giggling long enough to breathe.

Eloy and Simon came over the next morning. Mom and Hollie had helped Will get together the ingredients he needed, including lots of brown sugar and heaps of white chocolate chips. Both agreed he needed to do the baking himself, not because they were squeamish but because, as he'd said to Eloy, he needed to follow through on this part on his own. And maybe a little because they were squeamish. They worked on the banner and decorating the donation jars for the next day, while Dad took Eloy's little sisters for ice skating and a movie in Rochester, clearing the house so Mr. and Mrs. Herrera could work without distractions. Eloy said his dad went overboard in choosing recipes, as usual, and was already prepping like a wild man when Eloy left. With so many people helping Will in so many ways, he was determined to not mess up his part.

Which meant it was time to bake the White Chocolate and Wax Worm Cookies.

Will remembered seeing the recipe in the table of contents when he looked through David George Gordon's *The Eat-a-Bug Cookbook* online, but he was surprised when he did a Google search and found the recipe on Epicurious.com, a real website for real food normal people ate. Though Will was trying to show kids at school that bug food *was* real food, it was still a shock to see that others at a big American company had already figured that out. Will didn't kid himself that termite stew was going to become the next mac and cheese anytime soon, but the important thing was to start somewhere. So seeing the cookie recipe on an ordinary food website was encouraging.

Now it was Will's turn to start.

He got out the containers of what were technically wax moth caterpillars, tilting them back and forth to be sure all were dead.

"They kind of look like peanut halves," Simon said.

They didn't. They looked like frozen maggots with tiny black heads and six tinier black nubs of feet. Simon was being a good sport, but there was no denying that these "peanut halves" had once been squirming and wormy and alive.

"They're supposed to taste nutty," Will said.

"You should try one now!" Simon pulled out his phone. "I'll take video."

Will winced in Eloy's direction. "It's not supposed to be a joke," Will told Simon.

"I'm staring at five hundred dead, maggoty worms," Simon said. "Believe me, I *know* it's no joke. This is for public relations. We'll record stuff we eat to show people they won't die—or puke. Especially since you have a terrible track record with eating bugs and puking."

"I only puked once, and that was after a stinkbug *sprayed in my mouth*."

"Yeah, but you almost puked after the earthworm."

"Will you please stop saying 'puke,'" Hollie called from the living room. "You're making me want to barf."

"Puke!" Will, Eloy, and Simon all said at the same time,

cracking themselves up, while Hollie threatened to pour glitter onto their heads.

The recipe said it would be easier to pick out the wax worms from the wood shavings before they thawed, so Will and the guys got to work.

Simon kept trying to devise a way to pick out the tiny caterpillars without actually picking, bouncing the colander, or tossing handfuls of wormy sawdust into the air, telling Will and Eloy to swipe at them. It was funny at first, but then the worms got softer and softer. They were squishy and fragile, the skin so thin, it didn't seem possible it had ever held in the wax worms' guts. But they weren't popping between Will's fingers, either. They were tougher than they looked. Mostly.

Simon wasn't careful and broke a bunch in half, so Eloy gave him the job of rinsing off sawdust from the ones that had been sorted while Will and Eloy picked out the rest.

Until suddenly there was a damp, limp wax worm wriggling under Will's nose.

"Eat me," Simon said in a high-pitched voice.

Will batted at Simon's hand, but Simon pushed back, and then Will had a squished caterpillar mustache above his lip.

It felt like a glob of icing. But it wasn't icing. Will didn't move.

Eloy grabbed a towel.

Simon grabbed his phone.

Will tried to grab Simon's arm, but the camera clicked.

"You've got to see your face!" Simon said.

"Just give me the towel," Will said without moving his upper lip, eyes crossed as he looked at the white smear at the lowest point of his peripheral vision.

"You do look funny," Eloy said.

Simon flipped the phone around so Will could see the picture. He was almost as pale as the dead wax worm on his face.

"You know what will make it funnier?" Simon said, bouncing with a hand raised as if he was dying to be picked to answer the question. "Lick it off your face! People will go crazy."

Eloy handed over the towel but added, "It is an edible insect. You said that the farmer who raises them eats them raw."

"I'm trying to be serious about this," Will said carefully, the drying wax worm pulling on his skin. He gave Eloy a pointed look. Will wasn't sure he trusted himself to know the difference yet between fun and making fun, and he wanted to err on the right side of the line for once—and Eloy knew that.

"This one's funny," Eloy said.

"For you," Will grumbled, not fooled by Eloy's casual shrug. The guy was grinning too much.

"Just pretend to lick it off your face," Simon said, phone at the ready.

Will gave in. He crossed his eyes ridiculously hard, curled out his tongue as far as he could—and the wax worm fell right onto it.

His reflex was to spit it out, but he caught himself in time. The smooshed edges had already gotten a little crusty, but mostly the worm was soft. He didn't chew, just pressed it against the roof of his mouth, as if it was a glob of icing.

It wasn't.

He couldn't help being aware he was eating a wax moth caterpillar. But the wax worm really was nutty, like walnut paste. He picked up another one and ate it, to prove to himself he could.

"Don't eat all our profits!" Simon said.

"Your turn," Will said, holding out an extra-plump caterpillar. "You know you want it. Juicy worm guts are your favorite."

After he chased Simon around the kitchen a few times, both Eloy and Simon took turns eating one.

Eloy simply nodded. "It's good."

Simon rubbed his belly. "Mmm, braaaains."

"I'm going to need the kitchen back at some point," Mom said meaningfully from the living room.

The guys grinned at one another and got back to it.

Will remembered a few tricks from baking with Mom, and Eloy knew a lot of tricks. Simon was good for making a mess, but at least he was good for cleaning up, too. In no time, they had the batter ready with only the last step remaining of folding in the wax worms. Pouring them on top of the sugary dough made the wax worms seem extra wormy all of a sudden. Simon had suggested chopping them up so they wouldn't be so obvious in the cookies, which made sense from a culinary standpoint, too, but since the ultimate point was to show people that eating insects was cool, they saved a few worms and pressed them onto the top of the spoonfuls of dough before baking.

Waiting for the first batch, Will worried about his plan, though the smells of brown sugar and melting chocolate tried to reassure him. Insects *were* worthy of being normal food. But knowing that in theory and convincing others in real life . . . who knew? People would be there tomorrow, but would they pay for insect treats for any reason other than to be part of a joke? He wanted people to get it, to get that this was a real thing, but he was afraid he'd done too much damage with *his* jokes. No one expected him to be serious. Probably, no one *wanted* him to be serious.

Some of that worry went away when the first batch of cookies came out. They were good. Like, really good. Will and the guys ate a half dozen on their own. The brown sugar dough was crumbly, the white chocolate melty, and the baked wax worms even more nutty but also chewy. Maybe a little too chewy.

"We might have overcooked them," he said. The texture was a little tough. As the cookie crumbled apart in his mouth, the baked wax worms sifted out, leaving leathery bits of bug on his tongue. "I liked them better plain."

"You mean *raw*?" Simon said.

"No. *Fresh*." He really had liked them better when they were soft and creamy.

"They're just different this way," Eloy said. "We should make the cookies smaller so they don't have to bake as long."

He was right. The next batch was perfect. Mom was surprised by how much she liked them. Hollie tried one, too, but only one. Wax worms weren't crickets, but she was still a bit creeped out. Knowing how much the crickets had gotten to her, it was kind of a big deal that she ate one at all.

"What you're doing is actually pretty cool," Hollie said. "I really hope people get it."

That she'd named Will's own fear stung, but the fact that she got it helped.

Will had doubled the recipe, so it took a while baking cookies sheet by sheet, but it was nice, too. Will, Simon, and Eloy quickly got into a routine, and during breaks checked out Mom and Hollie's projects. They all agreed the banner was cool but told Hollie she had a glitter problem and had to run away when she blew some at them.

They'd just transferred the last cookies to the cooling rack when Dad got back from the city. He waved Simon and Eloy to come on for their rides home. When Will walked out with them, he saw why Dad hadn't gotten out of the truck:

Eloy's sisters were conked out in back, held up only by their seat belts.

Eloy blinked at Will's dad in surprise and respect. "They *never* stop when I have to babysit them."

From Dad's grin, Will knew he'd had a blast with the girls, too.

Simon called shotgun—quietly—and hopped into the front seat while Eloy hung back.

"Hey, uh, it was cool," Eloy said. "Hanging out with you guys."

When Eloy said, "you guys," Will couldn't help picturing who "you guys" used to be.

Only a few weeks ago, Darryl would have been there, as he'd been there before making chocolate chip cookies with Will and his mom or doing some project for school. Though Will knew it wasn't *all* his fault, he was part of the reason Darryl wasn't there. That whole earthworm-jerky thing. He let out a huge sigh. "Crap. I have to apologize to him, don't I?"

"Huh?"

"Darryl."

"Oh." Eloy squinted at Will. "He doesn't seem like a very forgiving kind of person."

"No," Will admitted. "But it's kind of more about me than him."

Eloy nodded as if he understood, and Will thought he

probably did. Some apologies would never fix things, but that didn't mean they shouldn't be made. It just meant they'd be harder to get out.

He sighed again.

Eloy patted his shoulder. "Do you need to hug me again?"

Will managed a quick headlock before Dad said if they woke the girls, he'd show them what a *real* headlock was.

SATURDAY MORNING WILL WOKE WITH A CRICKET sharing his pillow, chirping like a cheerleader. He left the cricket to enjoy the warm bed while he got ready for the tournament. They had to be at school by 8:00 A.M. to set up the main gym, but he wanted to get there early to set up tables for the Buck-a-Bug fund-raiser.

Light was just fuzzing the edges of dawn when Will and Dad swung by to pick up Eloy. Though Will was stuck with the middle on the bench seat, it was nice to be with a friend his age as they went to meet up with all the older guys on the team.

The ants had made Will's and Eloy's first official matches a joke. This tournament felt like the first *real* time he and Eloy would wrestle as Cobras. He wanted to prove himself, though the guys didn't care if he won or lost as long as he brought everything he had to the mat.

First he had to help roll them out.

Triton had four wrestling areas, which meant four matches could happen simultaneously so the tournament could move along at a good pace. But it also meant their mats took up so much space, the bleachers could be opened only halfway. It had never been a problem before, since usually only family and girlfriends came to tournaments, but now Will looked at the rows of unfolded seats and wondered if he wanted to need them or not.

He wanted Buck-a-Bug to do well, and he'd love to see lots of people come out to support the wrestling team, but if the event was a bust, he'd rather not have all of Triton on hand to make fun of him.

The guys were mostly quiet, still waking up, but by 9:00 A.M. the other four teams had arrived. The refs began weigh-ins and skin checks for the planned 10:00 A.M. start. When Trey and Max coached the refs to be extra careful about checking Will and Eloy for bugs, everyone perked up, a bunch of guys from the other teams already having been told about the fund-raiser and the story behind it.

Will supposed that was Coach Van Beek's doing, which was either a really cool thing to support Will and make sure the other teams weren't caught off guard or a not-cool thing at all because it greatly increased the number of people who might laugh at Will about eating bugs.

He lucked out when the match order was set to start with the 195 weights. A random draw determined the first weight class to wrestle, with the rest of the classes following in order. Starting with the heaviest class meant they'd loop back to the beginning for the second round, which meant lightweights Will and Eloy.

If they had gone first, everyone would have been watching them, and Will would have been even more nervous than he was. But going second was perfect. It meant there'd still be one or two heavyweight matches going on by the time he was up but that he'd have his first match done by eleven or so. There was a mandatory one-hour rest period after each one. Will would have at least two matches today, hopefully more if he wrestled well, but the match order meant he'd have a window of time right when he needed it for the promised noon start of his bug event.

Before Will or Eloy was allowed to put on his singlet, the guys made a big show about inspecting the spandex uniforms for ants. Will figured he was meant to act offended, but he couldn't pull it off with the goofy grin all over his face. A big part of him was nervous about what might happen in the next few hours, but right now he was just one of the guys.

The feeling lasted about three minutes. He left the locker room and entered a packed gym. Which he should have expected. A five-team tournament was small by tournament standards but big for Triton. There was a *crowd*, and it already included his family.

"I thought you weren't coming until eleven," he said to them.

"You're the one who kept saying that, dork-face," Hollie said.

"Of course we want to watch your matches, too," Mom said.

"How are you feeling? Nice and loose?" Dad asked.

Will had been so focused on bugs the last few days, he hadn't been very focused on the wrestling part. Back on that first day he'd met Eloy, Will had been reading *Wrestling for Dummies*, how wrestling in the right mind-set meant staying focused and mentally tough. He needed to remember that for the entire six minutes of his match. And he'd need to remember that even more at noon.

Mom pointed to where his grandparents were, so Will made his way up the bleachers to say hi. On the way, some guy, like someone's dad, asked, "You that Bug Boy?"

He surprised Will into stopping, and suddenly lots of people were calling to him.

"You really going to eat a scorpion?"

"Will the poison in the stinger kill you?"

"I can't wait to post it on my YouTube channel."

"It's disgusting. No one should let a child do something like that."

"You should be on one of those *Survivor* shows!"

Will turned his head toward each new voice, making himself dizzy. He wanted to be excited by the crowd's interest. He knew he should joke and tease and dare them to come out and try a bug for themselves. But he was too high up in the bleachers, surrounded by too many faces with too many words flying at him like a swarm of midges.

He started to feel queasy, and queasy was never good for him. He'd puked up the stinkbug and nearly puked after the earthworm jerky. What if it happened again?

He had been nervous but mostly feeling okay about his plan. Now, though, the feeling was very, very bad.

IF HE COULD HAVE CALLED THE WHOLE THING OFF RIGHT
then, he would have. Not because he was worried about
embarrassing himself if he puked, but because puking
would mean disappointing all the people who had
helped him.

He didn't remember doing warm-ups with the guys. He
barely remembered hollering with everyone during Randy's
match. He did remember Hollie frowning and snapping at
him, though he didn't remember what she'd said. It was like
he was in a cocoon, there but not there.

Then suddenly it was time for his match.

Dad, Pop-Pop, Mr. Herrera, and Elsi were on the sidelines
next to the mat, Elsi already hollering, "Squish him, Will,"
in her kindergartner voice. Even Will's opponent grinned,
nervously, at the fierce pipsqueak.

Will didn't. He heard her, but it was through the buzz
of everything else in his head. Coach must have been able

to tell something was up, because he pulled Will aside and asked, "You set?"

He wasn't. After this match, he was going to eat bugs to try to get other people to eat bugs, which would never happen if he puked. And then there was the scorpion. Jeez, he might not even make it to the Buck-a-Bug table; he might puke right there on the mat.

"Blink twice for yes," Coach said.

Will blinked but only as a reaction to being pulled out of his thoughts.

Coach Van Beek squared Will's shoulders and bent down to look directly into his eyes. "Take a breath." He waited until Will did. "Whatever's going on, it'll still be there when you get off the mat."

That was exactly the problem!

"The mat is where you get to let it go. For six minutes, you get to forget it. Channel the energy into what you came here to do. Relax, and focus on that one thing."

Coach was right in theory, but Will had never really needed to put it into practice until last week with the ants— and he'd tanked. And the ants were tiny compared to what was waiting for him this time.

Looking around, he spotted Eloy with Coach Taylor, readying for his own match. As usual, he looked serious and, unlike Will, actually *ready*, until Elsi shouted again, "Squish him, Eloy!"

Eloy was surprised into laughing and jogged over to her for a high five. He glanced at Will, a grin still on his face, and echoed her, "Squish him, Will."

"Enough with the squishing," Will's opponent joked, his good sportsmanship getting through to Will enough that he nodded at Coach and stepped into the central wrestling area.

He picked up the green anklet, his opponent taking the red, and strapped it on. The anklets helped the ref score the match, so they were important, but they could be annoying, because the Velcro bands fell off a lot. Will pulled his extra tight; he already had plenty of distractions.

At the ref's signal, Will stepped to the narrow rectangle marked in the center of the mat, taking his place at one end.

"All that squishing stuff," his opponent said. "You must be Bug Boy, huh?" The little laugh he gave told Will he was nervous, which would have made Will feel more confident if he didn't have a thousand nerves of his own.

"Her brother's just started wrestling. I don't think she knows the terms yet."

The guy only nodded, his Adam's apple making a big jump before settling again.

"Uh, good luck," Will said, reaching out to shake his opponent's hand. The handshake was how every match started, but not the "good luck." Will gave his head a shake, trying to let go and focus the way Coach had said.

"Yeah, good luck," the guy said.

They both crouched into neutral position, one foot forward, arms raised at waist height, facing off.

The ref's short whistle blast was like a lightning strike.

Will's opponent shifted down for a mid-level attack, stayed low as he took his penetration step, and grabbed Will behind the legs above the knees. The guy pulled up on Will's legs, spearing his forehead hard into Will's gut. Will grabbed at the guy's ribs to try to regain his balance, but the guy tucked his limbs close so he could drive his shoulder into Will. Will landed hard on his back, feeling the smack of the double-leg takedown through his entire body.

His opponent squeezed his arms to maintain control of Will's legs, digging his toes into the mat and driving his shoulders forward. He was so close to pinning Will.

What saved Will was Eloy.

It turned out Will's opponent was a lot like Eloy—stronger than Will but not as technically skilled. And Will had been wrestling Eloy for weeks.

His body moved on instinct and reflex, curling around the other guy and wrapping him from behind. Will rolled hard, whipping the guy's legs over his own head. On his back, the guy bucked to keep his shoulders from the mat, twisting and twisting until he was on his side and could reach to try to break Will's hold. But Will was still on top and in control, which meant he'd earn points for riding time as well as the reversal.

Will smelled the mat's fresh disinfectant and his opponent's forest-y deodorant. His ears vibrated with shouts from the crowd. Colors were sharp but shapes were not. His muscles roared.

On the mat, Will knew what he was doing. Even when he made mistakes, he knew how they happened and why, and how to try to fix them. But off the mat, when he made mistakes, what he did to fix them seemed like good ideas until he tried them and found out they were more mistakes. So how could he trust himself anymore?

In the too-long pause while Will's mind spun, his opponent managed to wriggle onto his belly and spread-eagle his free arm and leg to brace against another roll. After several seconds of stalemate, the ref piped a short whistle blow, breaking them up to reset in the ref's position.

Will got the bottom and sat on his ankles, hands flat on the mat in front of him, his opponent giving him time to set up before kneeling to curl around him. Will had practiced this so many times with Eloy, the whistle blow jolted him to action without thought. He grabbed the arm the guy had curled over Will's belly and used his weight and momentum to flip the guy over his shoulder. Will kept hold of the arm, rolled backward on top of his opponent, and grabbed one of the guy's legs. He pressed all his weight onto the guy, trying to get the pin, but his opponent was strong enough to fight his leg free from Will's hold.

The wrestling move was done, and Will was on to the next one before his brain caught up. The sequence forced him to see something: He didn't need to trust only himself. On the mat, he trusted his training, the coaches, and all the work he'd done with Eloy. Off the mat, he could trust his family, the Herreras, Eloy, and Simon. They were all in on Buck-a-Bug.

It didn't matter how other people reacted. What mattered was Will doing something he believed in. Doing it had made him feel closer to his family and strengthened a friendship that Will had learned was really important to him. Not that he'd say so to Eloy. Will probably already had to eat a scorpion today; he didn't want to suffer another headlock in Eloy's stinky armpit.

His grin confused his opponent enough for Will to make another takedown.

Will didn't get the pin.

But he won on points, and that was fine by him.

39

BY THE TIME WILL AND ELOY FINISHED THEIR MATCHES
and went to prepare for Buck-a-Bug, the concession window
was already open and several tables set up in the hallway. A
tournament day was long, so groups came out to sell everything from protein bars, muffins, and juice to pizza, chili,
and hot dogs.

Will had saved the best spot in the hall with two long
tables across from the concession window by the main
doors. Dad and Mom had hung Hollie's banner on the wall,
the one she had sprinkled all over with glitter. Will had protested the entire time she was doing it, but the sparkles did
make the words *Buck-a-Bug* stand out.

Mr. Herrera had gone all out with his supplies: large
white platters, fancy silver serving utensils, stacks of sturdy
paper plates, neatly folded napkins, and loads of plastic
containers. Although Will, Eloy, and Simon had made the
white chocolate and wax worm cookies, Mr. Herrera had

done the rest of the preparations. Will thought he'd make only *chapulines* and maybe one other dish, but Eloy's dad had done a *lot* more than that.

Along with a fresh batch of the spicy grasshoppers, he'd made familiar snacks with a twist. The "Chirpy" Chex Party Mix had crickets. The Rice Krispies Treats were sprinkled with termites. And then there were "Ants in the Pants": chocolate-covered ants.

That cracked up Will so much, he didn't hesitate to try a few. The ants crunched, tasting both bitter and citrusy, kind of like the rind of a lemon. They were strange, but with the sweet chocolate, somehow just right.

"I've been having fun with the bugs," Mr. Herrera said. "In Oaxaca, I remember mostly the *chapulines* and *chicatanas*, a salsa we made with flying ants when they were in season. But there's so much being done in professional kitchens now, I'm thinking of trying some specials at the restaurant."

Will blinked wide eyes. He was glad Mr. Herrera was happy, but Will wasn't sure how ready people in Minnesota were for eating bugs. He really, really, really hoped he hadn't set up Eloy's dad for disappointment.

"You could make anything taste good, sir," Will told him. "You could make my shoes taste good. Probably even my socks."

Mr. Herrera laughed. "I hope it won't come to that."

Will had set up the two poster boards he'd made about

the benefits of entomophagy along with a stack of flyers to hand out with more information. He'd also put together a special flyer for the wrestlers.

Always concerned about making weight, wrestlers were a perfect target market for bug eating. With more than 1,900 edible insects, there were tons of options for various nutritional needs: high protein, low calorie, high vitamin and mineral content. Mix-and-match insects were a great recipe for supercharged eating to manage weight, stay healthy, and build strength. He planned to take a stack of flyers into the locker rooms, too.

As he watched everyone get ready, Will's heart thumped as if it were too big to fit in his chest. All the people he liked most in the world were around him—Mom, Dad, Hollie, his grandparents, aunts, uncles, and cousins, Mr. and Mrs. Herrera, Elsi and Melanie, Simon, Eloy . . . and Darryl.

Darryl leaned on the opposite wall, hands in his pockets, just inside the doors as if he'd only arrived or was making sure he had an exit.

It was so unexpected, Will headed straight for him. "What are you doing here?"

Will winced, not meaning for those to be his first words. Surprise had caught him off guard.

Darryl crossed his arms. "Watching you embarrass yourself."

"I didn't mean it like that. I just . . ." Two thoughts clashed in Will's head at once.

The first was, he really wanted to stop having to say, "I didn't mean it like that." It usually meant he'd said something thoughtless or rude he had to apologize for, and he would *love* to skip both steps in the future.

The second was that Darryl was sweaty and wind-chapped, like he had ridden his bike to school.

It wasn't a terrible ride, about four miles with only the first short bit on gravel. But this late in November it was a *cold* one, and it made Will wonder if Darryl was tired of this feud they'd fallen into, too. A four-mile bike ride in winter was a lot of effort to make on the off chance that Will would embarrass himself, especially when Will was pretty used to embarrassing himself lately. Of course, putting ants in Will's pants had taken a lot of effort, too.

Will sighed. He wasn't sure what to think about anything Darryl did anymore.

"You just what?" Darryl said, his face windburn-red.

Will took a deep breath, wishing he'd practiced this. He hadn't expected to see Darryl until Monday. He needed time to think about what to say, especially because he didn't want to say any of it. Will knew why he had to apologize, but that didn't mean he liked it.

"I'm sorry. For the jerky thing. I was mad about the ants, but that doesn't mean it was okay for me to act like a jerk, too."

"Are you calling me a jerk, too?"

"Do you need me to? You put *ants* in my wrestling singlet." Seriously? Will was apologizing, and Darryl was going to give *Will* grief? Though, Will admitted to himself, the ants thing seemed so long ago. So much had changed lately, he could almost imagine a day when he'd laugh about it.

"It was only a prank." Darryl looked at the Buck-a-Bug tables, where Will's family and the Herreras were. "Not that it helped. You've gone crazy with this bug stuff."

Will looked over, too, where Eloy was helping his parents arrange food on the platters. "The bug stuff's cool. I wish you'd give it a try."

"I'm not eating a bug."

"You don't have to." Will sighed again, because he wasn't only talking about trying bugs, and he was pretty sure Darryl knew it.

People were already crowding around the tables, laughing and asking questions. Some of them came from the wrestling tournament, but Will recognized more and more faces from school, like Cristian, Tyler, and Joshua—people who had come out *because* of his event. It was time to get going.

Will turned to Darryl, and, seeing his wind-chapped face, Will knew Darryl had come out because of Will's event, too, and not to sabotage it or to see Will embarrassed like he said. Will thumped Darryl's arm, not hitting much through the puffiness of the winter coat he still had on.

"You know, one of the recipes Mr. Herrera made is called 'Ants in the Pants,'" Will said.

That surprised a snort of laughter out of Darryl, before he caught himself and rolled his eyes.

"Chocolate-covered ants," Will said. "They're good."

Darryl shook his head. "Like I said. Crazy."

Will only smiled and gave Darryl one last thump before leaving him to join the others.

It was time.

WILL HAD PREPARED A SHORT SPEECH EXPLAINING ENTO-
mophagy and reminding people of the fund-raiser part for
cancer research in Mrs. Graf's honor, but he didn't get to
say any of it. Too many people were already crowding the
tables, asking questions, handing over dollars . . .

. . . and eating bugs.

The first wave was a bunch of people from Will's grade
who had missed out on the *chapulines* the first time and
apparently didn't want to be left out anymore. After that,
a bunch of younger kids begged their parents for dollars,
loudly, and squeezed themselves forward the way only
little kids could. But quite a few adults gave it a go, too.
Dad chatted up the ones who seemed interested but were
hanging back, looking nervous. Mom, Hollie, Eloy, and
Mrs. Herrera could barely keep up with taking money and
handing out treats. Mr. Herrera kept getting pulled to the
side to talk cooking and bugs with chef wannabes and fans

of his restaurant, while Will kept getting pulled aside by wrestlers who had his special flyer in their hands. Simon stood on a chair over them all, playing the carnival barker: "Step right up and taste the food of the future!"

Wayne Graf, Mrs. Graf's son, made his way to the front, his half brother, Diggy Lawson, beside him. As soon as she spotted Diggy, Hollie pulled out a plastic-wrapped plate she'd set aside. Diggy showed steers and had won Grand Champion at the state fair last year, which meant he had money to spend and was famous for spending it at bake sales or on anything else his dad hadn't cooked. Wayne laughed when Hollie handed it over, because it was maybe the first time ever anyone had seen Diggy nonplussed by a plate of food. Not that it lasted long. He had a wax worm cookie in his mouth by the time he pushed his money into the donation jar.

In a shockingly short amount of time, the food was gone. Every worm cookie, every grasshopper, every single little ant. Will could hardly believe it. It had seemed like so much food—so many *insects* he'd thought he'd have to cajole people into trying—but he hadn't even gotten the signal for his next wrestling match yet, and the tables were picked clean.

The donation jars were filled . . . with a lot more than $250.

Which meant Will had to eat the scorpion.

Why had he agreed to Hollie's idea? Clearly, there were plenty of people willing to try something new. He doubted half of them even remembered the scorpion part of the deal.

But Hollie had. She stood on a chair, waiting until people quieted. "Thank you all for coming out today. My brother has done some stupid things. I mean, a *lot* of really stupid things," she said, going for the cheap laugh, in Will's opinion, and getting it. "But sometimes he does something really cool, like today." The back of Will's neck heated as an "aww" went through the crowd. "And now, what started with a stinkbug, ends with a scorpion. I've seen it, and, well, let's cheer my brother on!"

The crowd did cheer . . . until they saw what Will was supposed to eat.

In that Scorpion Scaloppine recipe Will had seen, the arthropod had looked like a scorpion-shaped chicken nugget.

Not this one.

Mr. Herrera pulled out a fancy white cake stand. He'd decorated the plate with curls of lemon and orange peel fanned in a circle and a light-green drizzle swirled on the edges.

The reddish-black scorpion sat in the middle.

Its body shone under the lights: bulging claws, central eye group, four pairs of legs, long tail, and curved stinger.

The scorpion was as big as Will's hand.

And it was a *scorpion*.

Will just kept thinking it over and over: *scorpion, scorpion, scorpion*. He couldn't take his eyes off it.

Eloy patted Will's back. "You've eaten worse." But he eyed the scorpion in much the same way as Will. They had ordered the "Edible Asian Forest Scorpion" partly because it was ready-to-eat, but it didn't look like it. It looked like it was *not* ready to be eaten and would fight back if Will tried.

"Omigosh," Simon said, squeezing Will's shoulders as if he were prepping his friend to enter the ring. "That thing's going to take your eye out."

"How do we put a filter on your mouth?" Eloy said.

"Admitting fear is the first step to overcoming it," Simon said.

"Is that from a fortune cookie?"

"A bottle cap."

Eloy opened his mouth but then only blinked at Simon.

Will laughed. His friends were ridiculous, but they made him feel better about what he had to do. A little. Maybe fifty percent better.

"Hey, look," Eloy said.

A bunch of the guys from the team were grouped by the table, calling out words of support and getting the crowd going again after their initial shock at seeing the "insect" Will would eat.

Will climbed onto the chair.

He reached down to the plate, wishing the scorpion weren't so . . . scorpion-y.

He picked it up by its tail.

Then he heard a chant from Hollie and some of her volleyball teammates.

"You can do it! If you try! Come on, Will! Eat that guy! Chew it up, chew it up. CHOMP! Chew it up, chew it up. CHOMP!"

His sister had written a bug-eating cheer for him!

Will grinned as he lifted the scorpion high into the air for all to see.

Lights blinked as photos were taken and video recorded. He held the scorpion at his open mouth and paused so everyone could get the shot.

Then he put a claw in his mouth and bit down.

It went so immediately silent in the crowded hall, Will bet everybody heard the crunching as loudly as he did in his head.

Because the scorpion was *crunchy*. The exoskeleton was shiny black body armor with not much else beneath it, at least not in the part Will chewed. It didn't taste like much of anything, but the pieces were sharp, so he chewed carefully. When he finally swallowed, so many people watched his Adam's apple, he swore he could feel their eyes on his throat.

When he opened wide and stuck out his tongue, the crowd went crazy.

Will raised his arms in a V and shouted, "I am Bug Boy! Hear me rub my wings together and chirp!"

Half the crowd picked up the chant, "Bug Boy, Bug Boy!" The other half chirped.

THE WRESTLING TEAM KICKED BUTT THAT DAY, FUELED BY
bugs and another unexpected bonus: Hollie had convinced
her teammates to learn a bunch of wrestling chants and
cheered on the guys, along with the massive crowd that
stayed after the Buck-a-Bug fund-raiser. The place was
packed with Cobras fans. It was totally cool.

Eloy won his second match and held out until the third
period before getting pinned in his third match. Will made
it to the fourth round, and the team earned enough points
for the overall tournament win. Afterward, Will went to sit
in the bleachers with Eloy and Simon. The three of them
leaned back and enjoyed the view from above, people below
scurrying and grouping like colorful insects.

"You got people to eat bugs for real," Simon said.

"I think they really liked them, too," Eloy said.

"We did good with the bugs," Will agreed, then grinned
at his friends. "Now let me tell you about this corn fungus
I heard is *delicioso*."

Eloy put Will in a headlock.

Bug Appétit:
A Guide to Eating Bugs

WHEN I FIRST READ ABOUT THE UNITED NATIONS RECOM-mendation that people eat more bugs, I had two reactions: "I get that. It makes sense." And "Eek—bugs!"

Everything Will explains in his class presentation is true. The global population will grow significantly in the next several decades and food resources are already strained. Many insects are wonderful sources of protein, healthy fats, carbohydrates, minerals like calcium and iron, and vitamins like B1 and B2. But, "Eek—bugs!"

Like me, you've probably had to eat something because "it's good for you." But this time we're in luck because bugs are more than good nutrition, they taste great, too!

Please keep in mind:

DO NOT eat bugs without the permission of your parent or guardian.

DO NOT eat just any bug, like ones in your yard or park. They may contain pollutants and poisons like pesticides. Always look for bugs raised for human consumption. (Resources listed in following pages.)

DO NOT feed bugs to friends, family, or anyone without first letting them know what they are.

DO NOT eat raw bugs. All animals, including insects, have pathogens. They can make you very sick. Cooking them ensures safer eating.

DO NOT eat bugs if you have shellfish allergies. They may trigger a reaction.

DO try a bug more than once! It can take a few tries to develop a taste for something new. I used to dislike salmon and brussels sprouts, but now I really like them. I will never like eggplant, cucumber, or cream cheese—blech—and that's okay because we all have different tastes. Try a variety of insects until you find the ones you like best.

CRICKETS: The Starter Bug

Crickets are very friendly insects for first-time entomophagists (insect eaters), because they taste like whatever *they've* eaten. Most farmed crickets feed on grain, fruits, and vegetables. They also take on flavors well, so are great additions to everyday recipes like pizza, stir-fry dishes, and tacos. Crickets add crunch!

LARVAE: The Tastemakers

Larvae are some of the tastiest bugs out there because they are basically storehouses for metamorphosis. In order to have enough energy to transform, they must stockpile nutrients like protein and healthy fats, the same things that make your everyday food taste good.

Mealworms are some of the most popular bugs in the entomophagy community. Other great larvae to try are wax worms, fly pupae, hornworms, sago grubs, silkworms, mushi, and mopane worms.

ANTS: Bittersweet Symphony

Ants secrete formic acid, which gives them a taste kind of like vinegar or citrus rind. Because of their tart flavors, they are tasty additions to salads or chocolate—and they make fantastic ice cream sprinkles!

For a special treat, search out honeypot ants. They use their bodies to store nectar and honeydew for their nests. And as their name implies, they taste like honey.

GRASSHOPPERS: The Heavyweights

Though grasshoppers may seem like large crickets, they have more "meat on the bone" and therefore a stronger taste, often compared to shrimp. Katydids and locusts are other grasshopper types and, because they are generally large and sturdy, they are great for kabobs or roasting over a campfire.

SPIDERS AND SCORPIONS: The Not-Bugs

Though spiders and scorpions are not actually bugs, neither are *any* of the "bugs" I've listed so far! To an entomologist, the previous are all *insects* from different scientific orders, like Orthoptera (crickets and grasshoppers) and Hymenoptera (ants). True bugs have their own order: Hemiptera.

But spiders and scorpions aren't from the scientific class Insecta either. They are both part of the class Arachnida. Though not insects, they are tasty, especially when served fried and on a stick.

TRUE BUGS: The Bugs of Bugs

To eat a *true* bug, there are several great options. Cicadas spend most of their lives underground, but when they do emerge they are tender and juicy, said to be meaty. In contrast, giant water bugs tend to be fruity, said to taste like a green apple Jolly Rancher.

What a stinkbug tastes like seems to depend on the person. I've heard "apple," "cinnamon," and "nothing much, it's more about the texture, like pumpkin seeds." So you'll have to decide this one on your own—just don't eat one like Will did: raw and after it's had time to spray in your mouth!

For helpful descriptions of how these bugs taste, check out *Girl Meets Bug* at edibug.wordpress.com/list-of-edible -insects/. *Little Herds*, at littleherds.org, is also a fantastic resource for anyone interested in entomophagy.

If you're not quite ready to eat a bug that *looks* like a bug, cricket and mealworm flours are readily available online and are wonderful for making things like pancakes and banana bread.

Bug appétit!

Bug Appétit: Recipes

When you are ready to begin your entomophagy adventures, *The Eat-a-Bug Cookbook* is a great place to start because it includes recipes, resources, and useful tips. Here are three recipes from its author, David George Gordon. Remember to ask your parent or guardian for permission to prepare these recipes. Also ask them for help with using the stove and oven.

Cricket Snack Mix

Yield: 6 servings

6 tablespoons butter or margarine

4 tablespoons Worcestershire sauce

8 cups assorted Chex cereals (corn, wheat, and rice) or
other dry, unsweetened cereals

1 cup Goldfish or other bite-size crackers

1 cup pretzel sticks, broken into small (1/2-inch) pieces

2 cups whole roasted crickets

Salt, garlic powder, curry powder or other seasonings

1. Preheat oven to 275°F.
2. In a small pan, melt the butter and Worcestershire sauce.
3. In a nonstick roasting pan, combine the Chex, Goldfish crackers, and pretzel sticks.
4. Bake in the oven for one hour, stirring every 15 or 20 minutes, until mix is lightly browned.
5. Add whole roasted crickets and continue to bake for an additional 10 minutes.
6. Remove pan from oven using an oven mitt. Season the mixture to taste and allow to cool before serving.

Chocolate-Covered Ants

Yield: 10 or 12 candies

8 ounces chocolate chips
1/2 cup (1 stick) butter
1 tablespoon corn syrup
3 cans (about 1/2 ounce) black ants

1. In a double boiler, bring water to a simmer. Stir together chocolate, butter, and corn syrup.
2. When all ingredients are evenly blended, carefully remove the double boiler from the stove. **It will be very hot.** Let the mixture cool to about 90°F. You can use a candy thermometer to measure the melted chocolate's temperature. If you don't have a candy thermometer, coat the back of a spoon with chocolate and place it in the fridge. If it hardens within 1–2 minutes, you're set.
3. On a sheet of waxed or parchment paper, drip small amounts of the melted chocolate mixture to make 10 or 12 quarter-size disks.
4. Before the chocolate hardens, add a sprinkling of ants to each disk. Cover the ants with the remaining chocolate. Refrigerate until firm.
5. After the chocolate has set, use a spatula to transfer each chocolaty disk to a plate. They are now ready to serve.

Wax Worm Cookies

Yield: about 2 dozen cookies

  1/2 cup (about 200) wax worms
  1 cup butter, softened
  1 cup granulated sugar
  1 cup packed brown sugar
  2 large eggs
  2 teaspoons vanilla extract
  1/2 teaspoon salt
  3 cups all-purpose flour
  1 teaspoon baking soda

Freeze wax worms overnight, then separate from their packing medium (usually pine shavings or sawdust). They are easier to separate before they thaw, so work quickly.

1. Preheat oven to 375°F.
2. In a large mixing bowl, cream together butter, granulated sugar, and brown sugar until smooth.
3. Beat in the eggs one at a time, then stir in vanilla.
4. Stir in all-purpose flour, salt, and baking soda.
5. Gently fold in the wax worms until they are uniformly distributed in the dough.
6. Drop the batter by rounded teaspoonfuls, onto non-stick baking sheets. Keep the cookies small. The larger they are, the longer the baking time, which makes the wax worms tough.

7. Bake for 8 to 12 minutes, until cookies are lightly browned.

8. Remove from oven using an oven mitt and allow to cool for 2 minutes. Using a spatula, transfer cookies to a wire rack. After they have completely cooled, serve.

Bug Appétit: Resources

Your local health food or grocery stores may have some edible insects in stock, but it is more likely you will have to purchase supplies online. **REMEMBER: Always look for insects raised for human consumption.** Here are a few websites to try:

Aketta at aketta.com
Don Bugito at donbugito.com
Ento Market at edibleinsects.com
Entomo Farms at entomofarms.com
Marx Pantry at marxpantry.com
Merci Mercado at mercimercado.com
Thailand Unique at thailandunique.com

Acknowledgments

THIS BOOK WOULD NOT EXIST WITHOUT THE TOWN-SIZE group of people who helped me in so many ways. I rub my wings together and chirp for all of you!

My parents, Teri and Duane, without whom this book would never have been finished; and Jesika, my favorite sister of all.

Melanie, Cristian, Elsi, and Tyler, middle-school students in Minnesota who read an early draft and called it "Bugtastic!" And to Rocio Gonzalez for organizing us.

Claudia Guadalupe Martinez, for a thorough and thoughtful sensitivity read that understood Will was meant to be a bonehead, but maybe not so big a bonehead. And Teresa Mlawer, whose later sensitivity read was encouraging and ensured I correctly translated "flaming butt of doom."

Christina Socha of Bugs Inc., Kevin Bachhuber of Big Cricket Farms, and Stacie Goldin of Entomo Farms, for answering questions about entomophagy as a personal pursuit and a business. And David George Gordon for literally writing the book about eating bugs, and providing tasty recipes for this one.

Coach Shane Van Beek and the Triton wrestling team, for not being too weirded out when I went to practice and a tournament with them. The young men generously answered numerous questions not only about techniques and rules but also about why they wrestled—their answers often personal and always sincere.

Triton Middle School principal Mark Raymond welcomed me to his school, secretary Joan Henderson made sure the visit went smoothly, and Mackala, Megan, and the seventh-grade class made my day as a student memorable and fun.

Amy Robinette quickly arranged a Skype visit for me with her sixth-grade language arts class at North East Carolina Preparatory School after her student Erick brought an unplanned snack to share—crickets!

Writing may be a solo activity, but it is a group effort in more ways than one. Thank you to friends who have supported me over the years, including Charli and Sam Martin, Eppy Camacho, Clem Camacho, Tom Boeker, Tracy Boyer-Matthews, Jae Brainard, Amanda D'Angelo, Lucy Potter, Yael Gold, Kerry Hogan, Sara Jenkins, Brenda Knierim, Kim Longbottom, Chris Power, Kristen Rudy, Deb Shoemaker, Jennifer Upchurch, and Marlisa Van Hout. And always to Caroline Kane Butts, an eternal inspiration.

Thank you to everyone at Bat Cave, especially Alan and Wendi Gratz. SCBWI Carolinas friends Carol Baldwin, Jo

Hackl, Bernadette Hearne, Lisa Kline, Jillian Utley, and dozens more who make our chapter so fun and supportive. The Wilmington crew: Chuck Ball, Emily Colin, Renée Dixon, Kathleen Jewell and the staff at Pomegranate Books, Birdy Jones, Teri Meadowcroft, Marilyn Meares, Catey Miller, and Dylan Patterson. The Boonies: Nancy Ashline, Robin Konieczny, and Elizabeth Rawls. Pitch Wars mentees Priscilla Mizell, Liz Edelbrock, and Jennifer Bryson, whose unflagging passion for writing invigorates my own. Ashe County librarians and staff for always being awesome: Peggy Bailey, Rebecca Kennedy, Laura McPherson, Suzanne Moore, and Marna Napoleon. And Debra Rook, who had the brilliant idea for a Buck-a-Bug fund-raiser.

Dana Sachs and Jaye Robin Brown, whose timely intervention saved the day at a low moment. Julie Sternberg and Michelle Brown, who gave me encouragement at just the right time.

Maria Ross, who copyedits everything I write without complaint—except for when I write "puke." And Sara Beitia, who kindly suggested someone offer poor Will a piece of gum.

My editor Howard Reeves's vision and patience made *Boy Bites Bug* a thousand percent better; and stalwart agent Kate Testerman never seemed squicked out by my idea, even when I sent excited emails about live cockroach cams.

Finally, endless gratitude to the Sisukas: Kathleen Fox,

Kami Kinard, and Jocelyn Rish. I am incredibly lucky to have these talented and generous women as my critique partners and friends. They never falter in their support, not even when I recruit them to help me prep and taste-test cricket tacos, wax worm cookies, and earthworm jerky.

For everyone, all that you wish for yourselves, I wish for you, too.

About the Author

While researching *Boy Bites Bug*, **Rebecca Petruck** prepared and ate cricket tacos and wax worm cookies from ingredients that arrived *alive*—and were delicious! The earthworm jerky, however, was *not*. She recommends juicy sago worms instead. Yum!

Petruck is also the author of *Steering Toward Normal*, which was an American Booksellers Indies Introduce New Voices and Kids Indie Next List pick, as well as a BCCB Best Book of the Year. It was also featured in *Vanity Fair*'s "Hollywood" column, the *LA Times*, and *Christian Science Monitor*. Formerly of Minnesota, Petruck now lives in the mountains of North Carolina. You may visit her online at rebeccapetruck.com.